FROM THE
NANCY DREW FILES

THE CASE: Find out who's framing Carson Drew for bribing a judge in a case of insurance fraud.

CONTACT: Ann Granger, the investigative reporter Nancy's father has been defending.

SUSPECTS: Judge Jonathan Renk, who is willing to betray an old friend.

Mr. Brownley, the taxi dispatcher who doesn't mind breaking the law.

Jim Dayton, the good-looking young cab driver who always seems to be around at the right time.

COMPLICATIONS: Someone desperately wants Ann Granger to name her sources, but she won't talk. Meanwhile, Carson Drew's entire career and reputation are on the line. Will Nancy solve the puzzle in time to keep her father out of jail?

Books in THE NANCY DREW FILES® Series

Available from ARCHWAY paperbacks

THE NANCY DREW FILES™ CASE • 15

TRIAL BY FIRE

Carolyn Keene

AN ARCHWAY PAPERBACK
Published by POCKET BOOKS • NEW YORK

AN ARCHWAY PAPERBACK *Original*

An Archway Paperback published by
POCKET BOOKS, a division of Simon & Schuster, Inc.
1230 Avenue of the Americas, New York, N.Y. 10020

ISBN: 0-671-64138-7

First Archway Paperback Printing September 1987

10 9 8 7 6 5 4 3 2 1

Chapter

One

I HOPE GEORGE has a good time," Nancy Drew said as she, her boyfriend Ned Nickerson, and Bess Marvin drove onto the expressway away from the airport.

"She won't," Bess said. She giggled, and her long blond hair bounced around her shoulders. "George hates ruffles—and that bridesmaid's dress is covered with them."

"Then why did she promise to be in the wedding?" Ned asked.

"George made that promise years ago," Nancy explained. "She was hoping Marian had forgotten it."

"So now she's on her way to Dallas," Bess said, an impish grin on her round face, "carrying a shrimp-pink gown with lace and ruffles and bows. Speaking of shrimp, I'm hungry. How about stopping somewhere for lunch?"

"Are you kidding? We just had breakfast," Nancy said.

"That was three hours ago!" Bess pulled against her seat belt so she could lean over to the middle of the back seat to see Nancy in the rearview mirror. "Pizza, maybe? With sausage and mushrooms and pepperoni and anchovies?"

"Arrgh!" Ned groaned and clutched his midsection.

"Forget the anchovies and it's a deal," Nancy said, passing a slow-moving pickup truck. "All right with you, Nickerson?"

He reached over and flipped a strand of reddish blond hair off her forehead. "Sounds great. Let's stop at the Pizza Palace. I can ask if they could use a hardworking college kid for two weeks." Ned was on a break from Emerson College.

"That's not fair," Nancy protested. "I promised I wouldn't take any cases while you were on break so we could spend some time together. You can work, but I can't?"

Her reputation as a successful young detective kept Nancy busy most of the time. All too often her job had meant she couldn't see Ned as much as either of them wanted.

"I won't be working twenty-four hours a day," Ned said. "And the important thing is, when we *are* together, we won't be out on some case chasing anybody around."

"And nobody will be chasing you," Bess said, referring to Nancy's most recent case, *This Side of Evil*.

Nancy shuddered. "I sure hope not." Taking the next exit, she headed for the Pizza Palace.

"By the way," Bess said, poking Ned in the shoulder, "George really meant it when she said you could use her car while she's gone."

"I'm still thinking about it," Ned said. "But if someone ripped it off while I had it—"

Ned's car had disappeared two days before. It had been stolen in broad daylight from the parking lot of a River Heights mall.

"Why would anyone want it?" Ned asked now. "It was five years old. It needed washing, and there was a rip in the cushion of the back seat."

"And a nail-polish stain on the dashboard," Nancy said, reminding him. "My fault for trying to fix a nail in a moving vehicle." She quickly glanced at his handsome profile. He wore a gloomy expression. "Don't worry, Ned. You'll get it back."

"Let's talk about something else," Ned said and sagged in his seat.

"Like pizza," Bess suggested. "With pepperoni and—"

Ned laughed. "Bess you're hopeless!"

By the time they reached their destination, it

was just past noon. The tiny parking lot behind the restaurant was full, but Nancy managed to find a spot at a meter across the street.

They lost Bess as soon as they got out of the Mustang. "Go on. I'll be right there," Bess said. Her nose was already glued to the plate glass of a shoe store. "They have sandals in already!"

Nancy and Ned headed for the corner, holding hands. Seeing their reflection in the window of a store, Nancy smiled to herself. Ned, six-foot-two and co-captain of Emerson's basketball team, had the kind of good looks that would turn the head of any girl. Nancy felt a surge of happiness thinking that their relationship had survived despite the demands her job placed on her.

They crossed with the light and started toward the Pizza Palace, which was nestled between an electronics/appliance store and a barber shop. As they were in front of the appliance store Bess caught up with them. "I saw two pairs I want," she gasped. "A bright turquoise pair and a white pair. They're great!"

Suddenly Ned stopped, looking into the window full of large-screen televisions. "Nancy, isn't that your dad?" he asked.

"Where?"

"There. Look."

Nancy looked into the store and saw tall, distinguished Carson Drew on all the various TV screens. He appeared to be leaving his office building, his arm in the grip of a uniformed police officer.

"I wish we could hear," Bess said as they watched a reporter shove a microphone under Carson Drew's nose on the nearest set.

"Let's go inside so we *can* hear." Nancy spun around and darted into the store.

A balding salesman hurried to her, but before he could speak, she held up a hand. "Please, we aren't buying. We just want to . . ."

Her voice trailed off as she saw the police officer put her father into the rear of a squad car. A tall, brown-skinned young woman got into the front seat. As the camera swiveled back to the reporter, Nancy crossed to the nearest set and turned up the sound.

"Hey!" the salesman protested.

"To recap," the reporter was saying, "Carson Drew, internationally known criminal lawyer, has been accused of attempted bribery."

Nancy's eyes widened. "What?"

"Drew," the reporter went on, "is representing Ann Granger, an investigative reporter for the River Heights Morning Record. He is alleged to have offered a judge ten thousand dollars to quash the court order that would force Granger to reveal the source of a recent story in the *Morning Record*. Granger's exposé uncovered an insurance scam run by members of organized crime. That's all for now, Larry. This is Jim Pratt at Judiciary Square."

"I've got to go to him!" Nancy said, hurrying from the store with Ned and Bess at her heels. "It's all a terrible mistake. My dad would never—"

"Of course he wouldn't," Ned agreed. "Hey! Watch it, Nancy!"

But Nancy was halfway across the street, darting between oncoming cars. Bess ran after her and tumbled into the back seat. By the time Ned had closed his door, Nancy was pulling away from the curb. One second later, and he'd have been left behind.

The police station was already jammed with reporters, cameramen, and newspaper photographers. Electronic flashes flared, and the quartz lights set up by the television crews exposed the faded paint on the grimy walls.

Nancy didn't see her father anywhere. At the moment all the microphones were pointed at the woman who had gotten into the police cruiser with Nancy's father.

"Who is she?" Bess asked. She was out of breath from the sprint from the parking lot.

"Dad's client."

"What will you do now that your lawyer's in jail, Ms. Granger?" a reporter shouted.

Nancy was too far away to hear Ann Granger's answer. She was edging around the crowd to get to the desk sergeant to ask if she could see her father.

6

"Well, I don't know," the officer said after Nancy got to him. He eyed her uncertainly. "He's being processed, and we don't usually— You're his daughter, you say?"

"That's right. Nancy Drew. Please, I—"

The sergeant's face cleared. "Say, you're the kid who's the detective, aren't you? I've heard of you. Let me see what I can do." He disappeared through a set of double doors.

"You okay?" Ned asked softly, tilting Nancy's chin up to peer into her face.

Nancy nodded. "I'm fine. I just hope they'll let me talk to my dad."

"Sure they will," Bess said.

The interview with Ann Granger was breaking up. Waving further questions aside, Ms. Granger threaded her way toward the now-vacant desk.

"Ms. Drew?" The sergeant, peering through the double doors, beckoned to Nancy. "In here."

Nancy grabbed Ned and Bess's hands and hurried toward the waiting policeman.

"Excuse me, are you Carson's daughter?"

Nancy glanced back over her shoulder. Her father's client was walking toward them. A worried frown was creasing her smooth oval face.

"I'm Ann Granger. I'm so sorry about all this. The charge against your father is ridiculous! If you see him, will you tell him I said so? I feel as if it's all my fault."

The TV cameras had swiveled around to capture their exchange. Reporters were heading toward them.

"Ms. Drew, what's your reaction to the charge against your father?" someone called.

"It's not true, and that's all I have to say." Nancy turned back to Ann Granger.

Looking up into wide, dark eyes, Nancy liked what she saw. The reporter was clearly upset, and her defense of Carson Drew seemed to have come from the heart.

"Come with us," Nancy said firmly. Turning, she marched toward the double doors as if she had every right to bring the others with her.

Carson Drew was cleaning fingerprinting ink from his fingers when he glanced up and saw the four bearing down on him. In his perfectly tailored suit and dark tie, he looked calm and composed, but Nancy could see the strain in his eyes.

"Nancy!" Carson said, enfolding her in his arms. "I was hoping you wouldn't hear about this until I'd made bail. Hello, Ned—Bess. Ann, it looks as if you've got a lemon of a lawyer. Feel free to cut your losses and find another, if you like. I'll understand."

"How can you think such a thing?" Ann Granger protested. "You're my lawyer, no matter what."

Nancy's father smiled slightly. "I appreciate your loyalty, but I'm not sure I can still work to

8

your best advantage. Getting myself out of this will eat up a lot of my time."

"Dad, are you forgetting me?" Nancy asked. "You can keep working for her. I'll work for *you.*"

Drew shook his head. "I'd rather you didn't, honey. I've been set up, and I'm sure organized crime has a hand in it."

"Mr. Drew?" A young man in uniform stood at Carson's elbow. "I'm sorry, but your visitors will have to leave now."

Nancy gave her father a quick hug, smiling to hide how worried she was. "We'll be waiting for you."

"He might be a while," the policeman said gently. "This way, sir."

He led Carson Drew through a heavy door. It shut with a resounding thud, and that was the last glimpse Nancy had of her father.

Back out in the foyer, Ann Granger began to pace. "This makes no sense at all. Why has it all happened *now?* The court order, the death threats—the timing is all wrong."

Nancy turned pale. "Death threats! Are you serious?"

"Only a couple of them." Ann spoke as if she were used to death threats. "But why now? I've already written the articles exposing the insurance fraud, and I've cooperated with the grand jury—except for naming my source, of course.

9

The grand jury will be handing down indictments any day now."

"In other words, everything's all over," Ned said.

"Right. So what's the point? Why threaten me and frame Carson, especially with something as ridiculous as trying to bribe a judge?"

"They goofed," Nancy agreed. "Who's going to believe my father would do such a thing?"

"Nancy," Ned said, his voice gentle. "People will wonder. Don't forget, your dad's not accused of bribing just anybody. His accuser is a judge."

"Which judge?" Nancy asked Ann.

"Renk. Judge Jonathan Renk."

Nancy stared at her. "You must be mistaken! Uncle Jon would never do this to my dad."

Ann's eyes widened with astonishment. "Judge Renk is your uncle?"

"An honorary uncle. He's a very close friend of my father's. I've known him all my life."

Ann groaned and slumped down onto a bench. "That makes it even worse. The accusation is coming from a respected judge who's also a family friend? Even if Carson is cleared, his reputation will be permanently stained."

"And if he *isn't* cleared," Nancy said, "it means a jail sentence. My father will have to go to prison!"

10

Chapter

Two

N_ANCY_, A_NN_ G_RANGER_, and Bess sat in the police precinct's cafeteria. It was a dingy basement room filled with vending machines, but since it was nearly three, they were all too hungry for the decor to matter. Ned had already eaten and gone back upstairs to see how much longer they'd have to wait.

"I just don't understand it," Nancy said again. "How could my uncle Jon do this?"

Ann sipped her coffee. "Judge Renk's reputation is as impeccable as your father's. Maybe more so, since he's been around longer. He must really believe the bribe came from Carson."

"He has a good reason." Ned appeared behind them. Turning a chair to face them, he straddled it. "It's worse than we thought, Nancy. The police have a tape of a call your dad is supposed to have made to the judge, offering him the money."

"What?" Nancy stood up, almost knocking her chair over. "Then the tape's a fake!"

"It must be a good one," Bess said, "if it fooled the judge."

"Right. That's really scary," Nancy said. "But how could my uncle believe— Ned, do you have a quarter? I'm out of change."

He dug into a pocket. "Who are you going to call?"

"My uncle Jon. I won't be satisfied until he tells me he really believes my dad is capable of something like this."

Nancy walked upstairs to the first-floor hall where she had seen a bank of telephones. As she deposited the quarter, Ann, Bess, and Ned hurried toward her.

Her ring was answered immediately, and she recognized the lilting brogue of the housekeeper. "Hello, Mrs. O'Hara," she said. "This is Nancy. Nancy Drew."

There was a sharp indrawn breath. "Ah, Nancy, it's a dark day, isn't it? How are you?"

"Fine, Mrs. O'Hara. Is my uncle Jon there?" The only response was a long silence. "Mrs. O'Hara, please," Nancy begged. "You know how important this is."

"Aye, that I do, Nancy. But his honor hasn't been well, poor man, and this business with Mr. Carson has almost put him in his bed."

"I'm sorry, but he can't feel any worse than we do. May I speak to him?"

"He's not home. And he's not at the court-house, either," Mrs. O'Hara added hurriedly.

"What time do you think he'll be back?" Nancy asked.

"I don't know, and that's the truth. Whenever it is, he won't be taking calls. He's that sick at heart."

Nancy was determined not to give up. "When he gets back, would you ask if he'd see me? Please?"

A gusty sigh told her she had gotten past the first hurdle. "I suppose it wouldn't do any harm to ask. I'll call you and let you know."

"I'd appreciate it very much, Mrs. O'Hara. Thank you."

Nancy hung up, wondering if she could really count on Mrs. O'Hara's help.

She glanced at the clock behind the sergeant's desk. The afternoon seemed to be crawling by, and sitting around doing nothing made it feel that much longer. She wanted to get to work on her father's case immediately.

Nancy turned to the reporter. "Ann, I need to know everything that's happened so far. How about filling me in?"

"Sure." Ann sat down on a bench and crossed her long legs. "I got an anonymous tip to check out the Mid-City Insurance Company. I found out that there was no such company. The address was a room about the size of a coffin, with a girl who answered the phone. Connie something."

"I don't know anything about insurance companies," Nancy admitted. "But what's wrong with using an answering service?"

"Not only did Mid-City not have an office anywhere," Ann said, "they had no insurance agents."

"I don't get it," Nancy said.

"Someone who said he represented Mid-City Insurance hired Connie's answering service to take their calls. Once a day the man phoned for messages. If Connie received any mail, she was to send it on to a post office box. She said they got one large envelope once a week. That was it."

"Didn't she think that was odd?"

Ann snorted. "What did she care? It was a cushy job, and she was being paid well."

Bess looked thoughtful. "Maybe *I* should start an answering service."

"Why not?" Ann said. "Anybody can. Anyway, by tracing who paid Connie, and then tracing the post office box, I finally stumbled onto the parent corporation. That was where several names popped up. Names I'd seen before —all tied to organized crime and all on the board of directors of Mid-City."

Bess sat down. "It does sound suspicious, but I have to admit I can't see what they were doing wrong," she said.

"I couldn't, either, at first. But I managed to

sneak a look at the message log Connie kept on Mid-City. All the calls to Mid-City were from three local businesses."

"So?" Bess asked.

"There were *only* calls from these three."

"Oh," Nancy said. "You figured at that point that they were paying their premiums to a company that didn't exist. And that's when you wrote the articles."

"Right. And they launched the grand jury investigation."

"And you testified?"

"I gave them everything I had and was thanked for my cooperation. They dismissed me. Didn't even press for the name of my source—not then, anyhow."

"Why'd they change their minds about wanting to know your source?" Ned asked.

Ann looked bewildered. "I'm not sure. I had put the Mid-City thing behind me and was following up a lead on something else. Then someone left a message at the *Record* for me to go talk to a woman out at Crimson Oaks—that retirement village on Wilson Avenue. It was about Mid-City."

"Who was she? Why were you supposed to see her?" Nancy asked.

"I never found out. I was just leaving to see her when this man came in and slapped the court order in my hand."

"The grand jury dismissed you and then issued the court order?" Nancy asked with a puzzled frown.

"Yes. I haven't gotten anything done since."

"What did you tell the grand jury this last time?" Ned asked the reporter.

"Nothing. I don't know who gave me that tip to check out Mid-City. Even if I did know, I wouldn't tell them. They recessed to give me time to think about it."

Bess's eyes widened. "What are you going to do now?"

"Stand behind my First Amendment rights, which imply that a reporter does not have to reveal a source. If it means going to jail, I go to jail."

Nancy stared at her hands. What Ann had told her was interesting—but interesting enough to frame her father? Someone obviously thought so. And I have to find out who, she mused.

It was late in the afternoon when Carson Drew finally appeared. His face was taut and grim. "Hi, everybody. Sorry it took so long."

"What's happened?" Nancy asked anxiously.

"I've been arraigned and made bail. Let's get out of here. I've had my fill of this place for one day."

"What comes next, Carson?" Ann asked as they left the building.

"A pretrial hearing to decide if the evidence is strong enough for me to be bound over for trial.

They'll let me know as soon as a date is set." He drew in a deep breath of fresh air. "Let's talk about it tomorrow. All I want to do now is go home. Ann will need a ride," he said to Nancy.

"Just to the *Record,*" the reporter said. "If it's not out of your way."

Nancy dropped off Bess and Ned and headed for the newspaper. Her father was silent during the whole drive.

When they reached the *Morning Record,* Ann directed her to the parking lot behind the office, where a battered old Ford was parked against the rear wall. Nancy pulled up behind it.

Carson Drew unbuckled his seat belt and got out. "I'll call you in the morning," he said, helping Ann from the back seat. "We'll see this thing through together." He shook her hand, then stood watching as she walked toward her own car.

"Whatever I can do, I'll do," Ann answered earnestly. "Thanks, Nancy. Hope to see you again soon."

The sky was dark by then; the parking lot dimly lit. There were only a half-dozen cars on the lot, and none parked near the reporter's.

Moving with a long-legged stride to the old Ford, Ann dug into her purse for her key and stuck it into the lock. She seemed to have difficulty getting it to work, so Nancy flipped on her brights, hoping it would help.

The beam brought Ann's car into sharp focus.

Just under the grimy tailpipe of the Ford Nancy noticed a small square box, so shiny and bright that the Mustang's headlights bounced off it. It was much too clean to have been attached to the car for long. What could it be? Nancy wondered.

"Got it," Ann called as the key finally turned.

"Ann! No!" Nancy acted without thought for her own safety. She wrenched open her door and hit the asphalt running. Ann stared at her in amazement.

Without breaking stride, Nancy hurled herself forward and tackled Ann around the waist. They landed just a few feet from the car.

Nancy's timing had been perfect. With a deafening roar, the old Ford exploded in an enormous ball of flame.

Chapter

Three

"Nancy, Nan, girl, wake up."

Nancy opened her eyes to be greeted by a shaft of sunlight across her face. Rolling over to escape it, she groaned. "Ow!"

Hannah Gruen, the housekeeper who had been looking after the Drews for the fifteen years since Carson's wife had died, was perched on the side of the bed. "How do you feel?"

"As if I'd gone over Niagara Falls in a barrel." Freeing an arm from under the covers, Nancy peered down at her bruised shoulder. "Now I know how football players feel after a game."

Hannah got up and raised the blinds even higher. "At least you're in one piece."

"How's Dad?" Nancy asked, sitting up and wincing. She had hit the ground harder than she thought the night before.

"In better shape than you are—physically, anyhow. He left for the office at seven."

Tossing the blanket aside, Nancy got up. She glanced at the clock and gasped. "Hannah, it's after eleven! I should have been up hours ago."

Hannah folded her arms in her I-want-no-nonsense-out-of-you stance. "You needed your rest. I wouldn't have bothered you at all, except that I have a message for you and didn't want to wait any longer to give it to you."

"What's the message?" Nancy grabbed her robe.

"Miss Granger called from the hospital."

"What did she say?"

"Just that you were to phone her as soon as you got up, and by noon at the latest."

"What time did she call?"

"About nine-thirty. I told her you two were lucky you weren't toasted."

Nancy had no answer to that, because Hannah was right. They had been just far enough from the Ford to escape the ball of flame.

Ann had landed even harder than Nancy. She thought she might have cracked a rib, so Carson had insisted that she go to the nearest emergency room. The doctors had shipped her off to X ray and made it clear they wanted her kept overnight.

Carson had been knocked flat by the force of the blast. But he had been lucky because he escaped all injury. A shard of flying glass had sliced through his coat sleeve but missed his arm. All things considered, the three had been extremely fortunate.

A few minutes later Nancy went downstairs and sat at the kitchen table to dial the number Hannah had left for her. Ann answered the phone with an anxious "Hello?"

"Hi. It's Nancy. Sorry to be so late, but Hannah just woke me. How are your ribs?"

"Bruised, not broken, but they won't let me go yet. Tests or something. I think it's just an excuse to keep me here. How's your father?"

"He's okay. He's at the office. Do you need anything?"

Immediately Ann's voice became edged with excitement. "I've heard from my source again," she said, talking rapidly and softly. "He left a message on my answering machine. But I'm sure it had to be the same man, even though he disguised his voice by whispering."

"What did he say?"

"He has another tip for me, but this time he wants to tell me in person. He asked me to meet him at the Grand Cinema on Shepherd Street at the first matinee. It starts at twelve-thirty."

"Uh-oh," Nancy said. "I guess you're not going to be able to make it."

"I can't even sneak out. I've got a police guard now, and his orders are to see that I stay put.

21

They may even place me in protective custody, if I'm not in it already. Can *you* make this meeting for me, Nancy?"

"Sure. I'd be glad to."

"Terrific! He said to sit in the aisle seat, left side, next to the last row. And call me back as soon as you can."

"If you're still there, I'll come by the hospital."

"Great. I'll be waiting for you. And thanks, Nancy."

Nancy hung up and sprinted for the bathroom. She'd have to hurry to get to the Grand in time.

Carson Drew was coming in as she was leaving, his briefcase stuffed to overflowing. "Some reporters followed me to the office," he explained. "They were driving my secretary crazy. If my being there is going to cause chaos, I decided to work at home."

"Any word on the pretrial hearing yet?"

"Not yet. Where are you off to?"

"Ann's heard from her source. She asked me to meet him." She shoved her wallet into her pocket. "He has another tip, and you never know —maybe he knows something about what happened to you. Have you talked to Uncle Jon?"

Her father shook his head. "He's not in, or not taking my calls. I'm stumped, Nancy. I thought I knew him. Friend for twenty years, card partner once a week for most of that time—it doesn't make sense."

"I'm sure it's just a big mixup," Nancy said, although she no longer thought so.

Her father took her hand and stared into her eyes. "Nancy, before you go, you have to promise me you'll be very careful. After what happened last night, we know these people are playing rough and for keeps."

Nancy nodded. "They must be desperate. I have to find out what they're so desperate about. But don't worry. I'll watch out for myself."

"Promise?" Her father peered at her intently.

"Scout's honor. See you later." She kissed his cheek and left, hoping she wasn't wasting valuable time on this errand for Ann. If the man's information turned out to be of no use to her in helping to clear her father, her next move would be toward the far side of town. She'd camp on the doorstep of Judge Jonathan Renk if she had to, but she would not leave until she saw him. He held her father's future in his hands.

The Grand was an old movie house living out its last days by showing film classics at discount rates to college students and senior citizens. Nancy paid for her ticket and went in. The movie, *Sons of the Desert,* starring Laurel and Hardy, had just begun.

Nancy slipped into the aisle seat on the left in the next-to-last row. Then she looked around. There were no more than a dozen people in there, most of them down in front close to the screen. No one moved, and no one checked to see if she had arrived. She hoped Ann's contact wouldn't be long.

Nancy loved Laurel and Hardy, and before long she was caught up in the film. Every now and then she glanced around, but no one approached her. No one seemed the least bit interested in her.

One-thirty, and Ann's source still hadn't arrived. He isn't coming, Nancy thought. She had mixed feelings. She was disappointed, both for Ann and herself, but she was also a little relieved. It was hard not to be nervous at the thought of what this meeting might have been like.

Nancy shifted in her seat, relaxed, and gave the two funnymen her undivided attention. The movie was almost over, and she wanted to enjoy the rest of it. So the hand that clamped over her mouth came as a complete surprise. And so did the icy barrel of the gun against the back of her neck.

"Well, well. Who do we have here?" a voice whispered. "You're Drew's kid, aren't you? I saw you on the TV news this morning. You aren't who I was expecting—but you'll do. In fact, you'll do just fine."

Chapter

Four

NANCY TRIED TO slip from the man's grasp
—and instantly regretted it. He tightened his
grip painfully.

"Make the wrong move, and the last thing
you'll see will be one fat guy and one skinny guy
hiding from their wives. Understand?"

Nancy nodded, forcing herself to stay calm.
She had to keep cool and carefully watch for a
time to escape. Then she realized she wouldn't be
able to watch anything. The man was slipping a
blindfold over her eyes. Then he slapped a strip
of adhesive tape across her mouth. Pushing her
forward in her seat, he tied her hands behind her
back.

"Okay, now, little lady, we're leaving," he
hissed. "Let's go."

Nancy wondered desperately whether any of the people in the front rows had noticed what was going on, but it seemed that she and her captor weren't attracting any attention at all.

Yanking Nancy to her feet, her captor led her up the aisle a few feet and turned right. Nancy had checked out the theater and the surrounding area just after she parked her car. She was sure the man was taking her out a side door to an alley. When a soft breeze brushed past her cheek and ruffled her hair, she knew she had guessed correctly.

She heard a car door opening. "Head down," the man barked, and pushed her forward. "On the floor, and no tricks."

Moving carefully, Nancy wedged herself into the space between the front seat and back seat. Then her captor slammed the door.

The floor felt gritty, and the interior smelled musty and old. Nancy struggled to find a more comfortable position.

"Hope you're cozy back there," the man said nastily. "I don't want damaged goods—yet."

Nancy's mouth went dry. Her mind was racing. Who was this guy? Nancy decided he couldn't be the same person who had given Ann that first tip. Ann said she didn't know who that man was, so she was not a danger to him. He'd have had no reason to kidnap the reporter. Ann had just believed him when he said he was the same person.

The engine coughed, rattled, then roared to life. Nancy waited until she was sure there was no one else in the car with them. Then she began to rub her temple stealthily against the edge of the back seat, trying to move the blindfold enough to see a little. It seemed like ages before she got a glimpse of the worn rubber mat she was lying on. It wasn't much, barely better than nothing.

Then she went to work on her bonds. The man had done a sloppy job. One of the knots gave a little, freeing a six-inch length of cord between her wrists.

Suddenly a radio crackled to life, and Nancy froze. After a few seconds, Nancy realized it was a CB. Her captor began talking so softly that she had to strain to hear.

"Lucked out. Granger didn't show, but guess who did? Drew's daughter."

"His daughter! Hey, wait, Wes—"

"No names! The kid's not deaf."

"Oh. Yeah. Are you sure taking her is smart?"

"Very. When we call him and offer to exchange his baby girl for the name of Granger's source, what do you think he's going to do?"

Nancy stiffened. How stupid she had been!

"Suppose Granger hasn't told Drew the name?" the voice on the radio said. "Reporters are funny about stuff like that."

"If she hasn't, she will now. Especially if she knows this kid's life is in her hands."

Nancy wasted no more time. She hadn't been sure why she was being abducted—now she knew. There was no way she'd allow herself to be used against Ann and her father. She had to get her hands free and escape!

Face up on the floor, Nancy arched her spine until she was supporting her weight on the back of her neck and shoulders and the balls of her feet. She lowered her hands past her thighs until her fists were behind her knees. That was the easy part.

Then, knees to her chin, she inched her hands under her feet and over the toes of her running shoes. After a few minutes of struggle, her hands were in front of her at last.

"Stop that wiggling around back there, or I'll stuff you in the trunk!" the man said, warning her.

She'd have to move more cautiously. Gently Nancy tugged off the blindfold, then stripped the tape from her mouth. She had been right about the condition of the car. The fabric on the back seat was split in several places, and the shield over the ceiling light was broken in half.

Using her teeth, she loosened the remaining knots at her wrists. Then it was just a matter of waiting for her chance.

After several minutes the car slowed. Nancy's heart began to pound. If her abductor had reached his destination, and there were others around . . .

Inch by inch, she lifted her head just enough to peek out the front window. He had just been caught by a red light! It was now or never.

Nancy jumped forward and delivered a hard karate chop to the side of the man's neck. But she must not have hit him squarely. As she opened the back door to jump out, he was fumbling with the handle of his door. She had only stunned him!

He was scrambling to get out, but Nancy was too quick for him. She threw her full weight against his open door and slammed it on his fingers. She saw his face contort with pain before she took off.

Nancy looked quickly around. She was somewhere downtown, but she couldn't tell where exactly. She dashed around the corner, where the traffic was heavier, and scanned the block frantically for a blue uniform or a squad car. But there were none in sight. Nancy kept running until she saw a man getting out of a cab.

"Taxi!" she yelled and darted toward it. It seemed like forever before the cab's passenger retrieved his briefcase from the back seat and paid his fare. Nancy was terrified that she might be seen. But finally the passenger was gone, and she was safely in the cab.

"Where to?" the driver asked, turning around.

Nancy found herself staring into the brightest blue eyes she had ever seen, causing her to hesitate. The sunlight streaming through the taxi's window made the driver's thick, light hair shine.

Quickly regaining her composure, her first thought was to go to the movie house, to get her car and then go to the police.

"The Grand Cinema on Shepherd, please."

"You got it." The driver pulled away from the curb and reached for the mike hanging from the dashboard. "Two-nine-seven," he said into it.

"Go ahead, two-nine-seven."

Nancy frowned. The dispatcher sounded very much like the man she'd heard over the CB in the other car. Perhaps it hadn't been a CB, but a two-way radio like this one. There'd been no cab light on the roof of that car, but considering how beatup it had been, it might have been a taxi at one time.

"Two-nine-seven going to the Gr—"

"Wait." Nancy stopped him, speaking softly.

"Say again, two-nine-seven," the dispatcher said. "You cut yourself off."

"Where would you like to go, miss?" the cab driver asked. He sounded a bit exasperated.

"Make that Fifth and Cranston," Nancy said. She listened carefully as the dispatcher acknowledged the driver and signed off.

She wasn't absolutely certain it was the same voice she had heard on the radio in the other car, but she couldn't afford to take the chance. Her kidnapper might have told the man the place she had escaped from. All the dispatcher needed to hear was a cabbie report from that same vicinity that he was taking a fare to the Grand Theater, and he'd know Nancy Drew was his passenger.

The trip was a long one and the traffic heavy. Nancy kept glancing behind her until she was certain they hadn't been followed. By the time she got out at Fifth and Cranston, her pulse was normal again.

And she made sure she checked the name on the side of the cab before it drove away. Gold Star Cab Company. A name to remember. And a face to remember, too, she thought, suddenly feeling guilty. She was already dating the best-looking guy in River Heights—Ned Nickerson. Although Jim Dayton, the name Nancy noticed on the cab driver's license, did come pretty close.

Nancy turned her thoughts back to the mystery. Why would a cab company be part of a plot to kidnap Ann? And why had the voice on that radio recognized her father's name when he heard it?

She had learned something. She just wasn't sure what.

She'd learned something else, too—a very expensive lesson. She could be used as a weapon against her father.

31

Chapter

Five

THE TAXI RIDE had given Nancy a lot of time to think. She didn't dare go back to the theater. Her kidnapper was no idiot. He would have guessed that she had driven to the Grand and would go back for her car. He'd probably be waiting for her. She'd have to leave the car there for a while.

Then Nancy remembered she wanted to try to see her uncle Jonathan Renk. She could phone the police from his house.

She hunted until she found another cab—not a Gold Star—and took it to the dignified old section of town where the judge lived in a large white house.

"Something's going on," the cabbie said as they approached the front gate of the house. "I don't think they'll let me in there."

It looked as if every reporter in town was camped along the street. A policeman sat in a squad car blocking the gate, and a second stood guard on the sidewalk.

Nancy was starting to say she'd get out right there when she noticed the reporters turning to stare into the taxi.

Quickly Nancy gave the cabbie directions to the rear entrance. Then she paid him and got out. The back gate was closed, too, but she buzzed the house from the intercom hidden in one of the brick pillars.

"It's me—Nancy," she told Mrs. O'Hara. After a two-second pause, the gate clicked open.

The housekeeper was waiting for her and drew her into the kitchen. Before Nancy had a chance to ask to use the phone, Mrs. O'Hara said, "The judge is in the library. He knew you'd come today." She patted Nancy's cheek. "I'm glad you're here. I've had the devil's own time getting him to eat. With you here, I have an excuse to serve a small snack. Perhaps he'll take a mouthful or two to be sociable."

"This isn't exactly a social call," Nancy said.

"I know. But be kind to him. He's a good man."

He had been, once, Nancy thought. Now she wasn't so sure.

She hesitated. What about talking to the police? She should do it—but the man who had

33

abducted her was probably long gone. She had better see the judge while he was willing.

She was leaving the kitchen when the housekeeper's voice stopped her.

"Nancy, your father. Tell him Katie O'Hara sends her regards, will you?"

Nancy responded with a smile of gratitude and headed for the library.

At her first sight of Jonathan Renk, her heart lurched. He looked terrible sitting behind his desk. A small man normally, the judge seemed to have shrunk to be only a miniature of his former self. Dark circles ringed his eyes, and his skin looked slack and loose, like an old suit grown large because its owner had been dieting.

He didn't see her enter, but he must have sensed her presence because his chin came up sharply. But then he relaxed. There was a hint of a smile on his thin lips. "Oh, it's you, Nancy. Come in, come in. I always forget how much you look like your mother."

Nancy needed no reminder of how far back his friendship with the Drews went. "Thank you for seeing me, Uncle Jon," she said softly. "Mrs. O'Hara told me you aren't feeling well, so I'll try not to be long."

"I'd be grateful. I was about to go upstairs."

Taking a deep breath, Nancy searched for a way to begin. "Uncle Jon, I—I realize that you would have to report a bribery attempt, but—"

"I should have known you'd appreciate my predicament," the judge said, a trace of his old spark appearing. "Our system of justice is under attack from all sides, all sides. We on the bench are obligated to—"

"Excuse me," Nancy said, interrupting him. "I meant that I wouldn't expect you to do anything else. But please tell me that no matter how it looks, you know my dad would never stoop to bribery."

The skin around his mouth tightened. "You can't know what a person will do until you've carried his burden, sat in his place."

"But—"

"I will say that Carson has always represented the best of his generation in the protection of our laws."

"And that hasn't changed. You know how dedicated he is. He would never bribe anyone, Uncle Jon. He's innocent!"

The judge, dwarfed behind the massive desk, nodded wearily. "Then there's no need to worry. It'll be proven in a court of law. Now, if you'll excuse me, I'm very tired. It's been a bad week. My Martha was buried a year ago yesterday, you know."

Nancy was startled. She hadn't realized it had been a year since the judge's wife died. But she couldn't let him go yet. "Wait, please, Uncle Jon. Just a minute more."

He pushed himself to his feet, supporting himself on the edges of the desk. "There's nothing more to be said."

"Uncle Jon, please! It was someone else's voice, someone imitating him on that tape!"

"Tape?" For a second the judge's eyes were vague and unfocused.

"I'm sure a voice analysis will prove it wasn't my father, but in the meantime, his reputation will be . . ." Nancy broke off and stared at him, a funny feeling creeping up the back of her neck. "You *do* tape your calls?"

"I—" Judge Renk seemed confused, uncertain. "Yes. No matter. It was definitely Carson's voice. He called me the day before yesterday, and—"

"When?" The judge's statement had triggered a memory—her father grumbling about a one-hour morning meeting that had lasted until almost ten o'clock that night. "I even had lunch and dinner brought in," Carson Drew had said. "I was in that room so long, I got cabin fever."

"You say he called you the day before yesterday, Uncle Jon? But I know he was in a meeting from eight-thirty in the morning until ten at night."

"Then he must have called during a break." He spoke hurriedly, as if he were running out of breath. "That's it, during a break."

"What time was it?"

"I—I don't remember exactly. I'll have to

36

think about it. I—" Frowning, he rubbed his forehead. "Maybe it was the day before that."

Nancy felt a stirring in the pit of her stomach as the beginning of a very unpleasant and unexpected suspicion began to filter through her mind.

"I'll have to check," the judge was saying. "I—" Suddenly his voice failed, and he shook his head. "Carson doesn't deserve this."

It came so softly that Nancy almost missed it. "'Doesn't deserve . . .' This is a frameup, and you're a part of it, aren't you?" Suddenly she knew it for certain, and the realization left her stunned. "You made the bribery accusation, knowing it wasn't true!"

The judge tried to bristle, but it didn't work. "I won't be talked to like this," he said, blustering.

Darting behind the desk, Nancy leaned over him. "You lied, Uncle Jon! Why? *Why?*"

"Please, you don't understand."

"Oh, Uncle Jon! What would Aunt Martha say if she knew? She used to say my dad was like a son to her! So did you! Yet you're trying to ruin him! He'll be disbarred, go to prison—"

"It won't come to that. I won't let it."

"We were almost killed last night! Ann Granger and my father and me—because we were with her! Her car was rigged to explode when she opened the door. She's in the hospital right now."

"No," the judge whispered.

"And about an hour ago a man tried to kidnap me. It was going to be a swap—my life for the name of Ann Granger's contact!"

The judge's face was pale. "They wouldn't."

"Why wouldn't they? They are capable of anything! It's up to *you* to stop them! You, protector of our system of laws!"

With his own words used as a weapon against him, the judge seemed to collapse. "No more, Nancy. I swear to you I never thought it would go this far, never thought—" He dabbed at his forehead. "Get the police, Nancy. I'll do what has to be done."

Nancy's sense of triumph was muted by a deep sadness. One of her childhood idols had crumbled before her eyes. "There's a squad car out front," she said softly. "I'll ask one of the officers to come in." She hurried from the room, afraid he would change his mind.

Crossing the marble foyer, Nancy heard footsteps. Mrs. O'Hara was just at the entrance to the library, a tray of covered dishes in her hand. "I'll be right back," Nancy called to the housekeeper.

"Hurry, then. It's soup, nice and hot."

As Nancy opened the front door, a shot shattered the silence behind her. She whirled around. Mrs. O'Hara, one foot across the threshold to the library, dropped the tray. Heavy soup bowls and spoons went flying—the crockery shattering and soup splattering everywhere.

Then the housekeeper screamed, a wail of horror that ricocheted against the paneled walls and pierced Nancy's heart with dread.

Mrs. O'Hara turned toward her, eyes wide and horrified. "Oh, Nancy! The judge has shot himself!"

Chapter

Six

THE NEXT TIME Nancy looked at her watch, it
was four forty-five, and the judge's body was
being carried out the front door. Mrs. O'Hara
had been mistaken. Jonathan Renk had not fired
the weapon himself. A neat round hole in the
window behind him made it clear that he had
been shot from outside. And proof of Carson
Drew's innocence had died with him.

THE NEXT TIME Nancy looked at her watch, it
was four forty-five, and the judge's body was
being carried out the front door. Mrs. O'Hara
had been mistaken. Jonathan Renk had not fired
the weapon himself. A neat round hole in the
window behind him made it clear that he had
been shot from outside. And proof of Carson
Drew's innocence had died with him.

The house and grounds were swarming with
police. Nancy felt as if she had been there for
days. She had told three different officers what
happened in minute detail. She had also been
fingerprinted to eliminate her prints from the
others in the room, even though it was obvious
the shot had come from outdoors.

Her announcement that the judge had been

planning to admit his part in the frameup had been met with raised eyebrows. The police had only her word for it, and that wasn't enough considering the situation with her father. Discouraged, she stopped trying to convince them after a while.

Now the pace of activity had begun to slow. Nancy sat near the bottom of the staircase and tried to sort out her feelings.

She had gone through her ordeal alone. Her father was in court. Ned was out job hunting.

She'd had to be the professional Nancy Drew and react to the emergency—checking for a pulse she knew would not be there, getting the police, trying to calm Mrs. O'Hara, answering the same questions again and again.

That phase was over. She could be plain Nancy Drew for a few minutes and feel the pain of her loss. Her uncle Jon was dead, a friend she had known all her life. And even though he'd proven himself to be less than admirable during his last few days, at the end he had shown himself to be a friend of the Drews, ready to do anything to clear Nancy's father. Her head lowered, her arms wrapped around her knees, Nancy let herself grieve for Jonathan Renk.

Finally the mournful chime of his grandfather clock reminded her of the time. She had work to do, a case to solve. And with her father's accuser dead, she was back to square one.

But first there was a nagging question to deal with. How was it that her uncle Jon had been shot immediately after he had decided to come clean? It was as if his murderer had been right there with them. Was it possible—?

Nancy got up and peeked into the library. Two men in shirt-sleeves were talking in a corner. Behind them a police photographer hopped around taking pictures, his flash attachment flaring. Nancy backed away and headed for the kitchen.

Mrs. O'Hara was resting in her room next to the kitchen. She was stretched out on her bed, eyes closed. Her television was on with the sound turned down.

"Mrs. O'Hara, how are you feeling?" Nancy asked gently.

The housekeeper opened her eyes and gave a weak smile. "Better, lass. Are they done? Have they taken him away?"

"Yes. Do you feel like talking?"

"Aye." Swinging her legs over the side of the bed, she sat up. "It's time I pulled myself together. There's so much to do. There are the funeral arrangements to start—"

"Don't worry. I've called Hannah, and she's on her way here. She and my dad will help you."

Dad. Nancy had been almost glad he hadn't been home. She didn't want to be the one to have to tell her father about the murder of his old friend. Giving the news to Ann and Bess had been bad enough.

"Mr. Carson would do that? Help with services for the judge?" the housekeeper was asking. "Even after everything—"

"Of course. He thought the world of Uncle Jon. Mrs. O'Hara, have any workmen been here recently? Perhaps someone from the telephone company?"

"No, there's nothing wrong with our phones."

"No strangers at all?"

"Not a one, until that crowd of reporters showed up yesterday morning. Pesky bunch. One of them had the brass to follow the cable TV man right in the back door. I told him what I thought of him, that I did. The repairman, too, until he told me who he was and what he wanted."

"You weren't expecting a repairman?" Nancy's pulse quickened.

"No. He said some kids had been tampering with the cable junction box out on the street, and he was checking to make sure they hadn't interfered with the pay-channel service—the movies and such."

"That was yesterday morning?"

"No, I'm wrong. It was afternoon."

"How long was he here?"

"No time at all. Maybe fifteen minutes."

"And you were with him the whole time?"

"Goodness, no. I was fixing the judge's lunch,

so I showed the man where the sets were and left him to it." She stopped when she saw one of the detectives standing in the doorway.

"Are you up to talking to me now?" he asked kindly.

He was just the excuse Nancy needed to leave. "I'll wait outside, Mrs. O'Hara." She had some searching to do.

The library was empty. The black dust of the fingerprint experts and the tiny hole in the window were the only signs that anything unusual had happened there. A television was set into the wall behind sliding doors. Nancy opened them and gazed thoughtfully at the big blank screen.

The channel-selector box was on a shelf beneath the set. It was small and rectangular, about the size of an answering machine. Nancy slid the shelf out until she could see the phone numbers of the cable company printed on a label stuck to the side of the selector. Unwilling to touch anything on the judge's desk, she went out into the hall to use the phone.

After two minutes of conversation with the dispatcher of the cable TV's service department, her suspicions were confirmed—they had not sent a repairman.

Nancy went back to stare at the set. She ran her fingers along the outer edges of the television, reaching as far into the recess as she could. There was nothing there, and the set was too heavy for her to pull out alone.

The shelf below was still extended. She slid it back into position, then remembered she hadn't examined the channel selector. She picked it up and looked at all sides. Nothing. She checked the bottom. Nothing. She had set it down before she realized she *had* seen something after all.

Nancy turned the selector over again. It sat on four rubber rings that protected the furniture from being scratched. About the size of dimes, the thick rings had screws in their centers attaching them to the base of the box. In three of the rings, the screws were visible. But in the fourth was a tiny, metallic cylinder.

She found what she had been looking for. The room was bugged.

Nancy went back to Mrs. O'Hara's room. Mrs. O'Hara's television sat there, the selector on top, a silent witness to the conversation between the housekeeper and the detective. Finger to her lips, Nancy beckoned them out to the kitchen and into the pantry.

"What's up?" the detective asked impatiently.

Nancy told him what she had found. "That's how they knew he was about to admit everything! They must have had someone nearby, just in case."

The detective's face told her he wasn't ready to take her word for it. "I'll go check," he said.

"And I let him in!" Mrs. O'Hara said tearfully after he had left. "It's all my fault!"

"You couldn't have known," Nancy said to

assure her. "When a man shows up in a cable company truck, you expect him to be what he says he is."

"But he didn't—show up in the usual truck, I mean." She pulled a handkerchief from her apron and dabbed at her eyes. "It was a white van like the one the cable company uses, but I didn't notice until he was leaving that it didn't have the purple letters on the sides."

"It didn't?"

"There was tape on the sides, long strips of it. Maybe there was a sign under it. I was busy. I just didn't think— And it had a bent front fender that ripped into some of the rosebushes as it came through the back gate."

"Ms. Drew?" the detective said softly, pausing on his way past the pantry door. "My apologies. You were right." He smiled. "Thanks." Then he was gone again.

Chalk one up for our side, Nancy thought and then turned back to the housekeeper. "What did the man look like, Mrs. O'Hara?"

"Oh my. Forty, maybe. Not tall, not short. Average, he was, wearing the purple cable company cap. That's all I really looked at."

Nancy decided not to pressure her to remember any more. The police would be doing that soon enough.

One of the officers who had been stationed out front interrupted them. "Excuse me, but were either of you ladies expecting a Hannah Gruen and a Bess Marvin?"

"Hannah's come?" Mrs. O'Hara rushed out of the pantry.

"It's okay," Nancy said to the officer and followed him to the back door.

There were two cars outside. One of them was Nancy's.

Hannah was lifting a cake carrier from the rear of her station wagon. "I baked a cake this morning," she called to Mrs. O'Hara. "Thought I'd bring it along so you'd have something in the house to serve to visitors."

"Oh, bless your heart." The judge's housekeeper pecked Hannah on the cheek and led her into the kitchen.

"Are you all right?" Hannah asked as she passed Nancy at the door.

"I'm okay." Nancy managed a smile for her, then turned to stare at Bess, who stood nervously in front of the Mustang. "How'd you pick up my car?" she asked her friend.

"As soon as you talked to me, I called Hannah and asked her to wait for me. She found the spare keys to your car and drove me to the Grand so I could follow her here in it."

Nancy hugged her. "You are a real pal. Thanks."

"Sure. I just thought that if it stayed there too long, somebody might steal it. Is there anything I can do? In there?" Bess nodded toward the house.

"No. Now that Hannah's here, she'll take over. Your timing's great. I was just about to call a cab."

After checking with the detective, Nancy said her goodbyes and promised to keep in touch with Mrs. O'Hara. As she and Bess drove through the back gate, she saw where the rosebushes on her left had been ripped by the van. Its fender must have been sticking out quite far to have done as much damage as it had.

Nancy poured out her worries to Bess about how much more difficult it would be to clear her father now. She wasn't paying much attention to the road—until a hard bump against the back of the Mustang alerted her to what was happening behind her.

"What was that?" Bess asked, turning in her seat.

"Some idiot is tailgating me at fifty-five miles an hour!" Nancy said. Her eyes flew to the rearview mirror, and she saw the ebony-tinted windshield of a dirty white van. It was so close that its front bumper might have been locked with Nancy's rear one.

"He must be crazy!" Bess said.

"I hope that's all he is," Nancy responded. It might be pure coincidence that it was a white van, she told herself. There were a lot of dummies on the road who got a kick out of driving recklessly. She sped up to put a little distance between them.

The increase in speed didn't work. The van simply closed the distance and banged her again, so hard that she and Bess were thrown forward violently. Only her seat belt prevented Nancy from hitting the steering wheel. If there had been a car in front of her, she'd have been pushed into it.

"Can you see his fender?" she asked Bess anxiously.

Bess peered in the outside mirror on her door. "Uh-huh," she said, her teeth clenched.

"Is it bent? Sticking out on the side?"

"Uh-huh. Do you know who it is?"

"Sort of."

There was no time to explain. The van was closing in for another attack. The driver intended to force them off the road and over an embankment. From there it would be about a forty-foot drop. Straight down.

Chapter

Seven

THINK YOU CAN get away from him?" Bess asked, her voice cracking with strain.

"Piece of cake," Nancy said and hoped she sounded convincing. They were in a tight spot, and it was up to her to get them out of it.

Fear had dampened her palms. She scrubbed one, then the other against her thighs to dry them. Her hands ached from her tight grip on the steering wheel. Drawing a deep breath to calm herself, Nancy settled down to outdrive her opponent.

"Hold on," she told Bess, who had braced her arms against the dashboard.

Keeping an eye on traffic in the lane on her left, Nancy darted into it the first chance she had. As she knew it would, the van followed. A tractor-trailer that had been behind the van in the right

lane sped up. Nancy glanced up quickly to see
the driver curiously peering over at them from
the cab of his huge rig.

A plan began to take shape in her mind. "Bess,
open your window and wave to that truck driver.
Hurry!"

Bess followed orders, her blond hair whipping
in the wind. "Uh—are you sure you know what
you're doing?" she asked in a nervous quaver.

The trucker edged alongside, and Nancy
smiled up at him. She wanted him to remember
them—and, if possible, supply a little help.

"Nancy, have you flipped?" Bess asked. "The
guy behind us is trying to kill us—and you're
flirting with a truck driver?"

The man grinned down at them, then tilted his
head toward the van behind her, his brows raised
in a silent question.

With one hand, Nancy signaled that she
wanted to get in front of him. He nodded. She
could have performed the maneuver without his
cooperation since there was enough room, but
having the trucker in on the scheme was an
added safety factor.

Flooring the accelerator, she shot ahead, then
slipped in front of the rig. It moved up behind
her, preventing the van from easing over between
them.

Very, very gradually, Nancy decreased her
speed. Finally the driver of the van had to pass
her: He was in the fast lane with an oil tanker

coming on hard behind him. A hundred yards farther, he moved over in front of her.

"Right where I want him!" Nancy shouted in triumph. With a beep of thanks to the trucker, she began to edge up closer to the van.

"What are you doing?" Bess shrieked.

"This guy left hidden mikes all over my uncle Jon's house yesterday," Nancy said. "It's a cinch somebody was listening when he decided to confess. They killed him before he could talk."

"You think the killer's driving that van?"

"It's a possibility. We know he's capable of it. He tried to kill us, didn't he?"

"Why are you chasing him, then? We should get off the highway and phone the police."

"I plan to. I wanted to have a license number to give them, but it's smeared with dirt. And I must have made him nervous. Look at him."

The van was edging back into the fast lane again, coming dangerously close to causing an accident. He sped up, changed lanes, and, without using his turn signal to telegraph his intention, zipped off at the next exit.

"*Now* can we go tell the police about him?" Bess asked.

"We're on our way. Maybe this time they'll listen to me," Nancy said. "This time I have a witness. And, Bess—you can close the window now."

* * *

By the time Nancy got home from the police station, it was after dark. There were no lights on in her house. Carson Drew had heard the news about his friend's murder and had left a note saying that he would be at the judge's house if Nancy needed him. Hannah was still there, too.

Bess lingered in the kitchen for a few minutes, wearing a worried frown. "I wonder where Ann is," she asked, fretting. They had called the hospital from the police station and been told the reporter had checked out. No one answered at her apartment.

"The police may have stashed her somewhere. If she can phone us, she will. Want something to eat?"

Bess looked tempted, but shook her head. "I think I'll head home. You've had a rough day."

"I'm okay," Nancy said. "I'll see you tomorrow. Thanks again for getting my car for me." Then Nancy shooed Bess out the door.

Before Bess got into her car, she looked back at Nancy and grinned. "Hey, I forgot to tell you —George called. She's having a ball."

"That's great."

"She doesn't feel so bad about her dress anymore. She said she still looks like a frilly giraffe in it, but the rest of the bridesmaids look even worse."

Nancy laughed. "Poor George."

Bess sobered. "I didn't tell her what was happening here. I figured it would spoil things for her."

"You did the right thing. Talk to you tomorrow." Nancy stood outside the door until Bess's headlights disappeared.

The dark house felt big and empty to Nancy. She wasn't frightened, just a little lonely and very, very worried.

The events of the day had shown her the kind of people she was up against. It was obvious they'd do anything to find out who had led Ann to Mid-City Insurance.

But what difference did it make who'd done it? The articles in the *Morning Record* had put them out of business immediately. There was nothing left to hide.

Or was there? "What if Mid-City was just the tip of the iceberg?" Nancy said out loud. Suppose the insurance scam was a part of a larger scheme? Suppose there was a great deal left to hide? It was the only thing that made sense. "What else could they be up to?" she asked.

Suddenly the doorbell rang. Nancy jumped. Steeling herself, she peeked out the window —and saw Ned's tall frame silhouetted against the amber glow of the streetlights.

Joyfully, she opened the door. Before she could say hello, he had swept her into his arms and was kissing her. Nancy returned the kiss eagerly. She decided he had just showered. His hair was still damp, and he smelled of soap and a woodsy cologne.

"That's the nicest thing that's happened to me all day," Nancy said when Ned lifted his head.

He looked down at her solemnly. "I'm not surprised, considering what you've been through. I'm so sorry about the judge."

"Was it on the news?" she asked, leading him to the sofa.

"That, and the fact that there's an all-points bulletin out on a white van with a twisted fender." He took a seat and pulled her down to sit beside him, nestling her against his side. "Are you all right?"

"I am now," Nancy said with a smile. She tucked her head under his chin and relaxed against him. "I'm glad you're here. Did you have any luck finding a job?"

"Nope. Hunting for a place that will hire me for two weeks is the pits. So far, I haven't found anything. The way things are going, I should hire myself as your bodyguard. No charge, either." He nuzzled her ear. "I love you, Nancy Drew."

Nancy felt so content that she was ready to purr. She and Ned had had their problems recently. They'd even dated other people for a while. But it hadn't felt right to either of them. Now there they were, together again. "I love you, too, Ned Nickerson," she said. "Probably always will."

"You'll get no complaints from me." Ned kissed her again, but broke off abruptly to exclaim, "Hey, is this a date? Have we finally managed to work in an evening together like a regular guy and girl?"

"That's what it seems like to me," Nancy said.

But Ned suddenly dropped his teasing tone. "I shouldn't have said that. You're not a regular girl. You're a detective saddled with the most important case of your life. Our date can wait, Nancy. You've got to clear your dad. Want to talk about it?"

"Ned, you're terrific. Yes, I do want to talk about it. Something just occurred to me before you came in."

"Let's hear it," Ned said.

Nancy began to talk. For a couple of hours she talked about the case. Ned was a good sounding board. His quick mind and active imagination fed her own ideas.

By the time she drove him home, Nancy was beginning to focus her plan. She was almost positive she was on the right track.

"I've got to be," she muttered into the darkness. She couldn't afford to be wrong. If she was, her father's career would be over—*and* she just might be dead.

Chapter

Eight

ANN GRANGER CALLED at seven the next morning.

"Where *are* you?" Nancy asked.

"Back home, over the strong objections of the River Heights Police Department."

"Why?"

"They checked me out of the hospital and wanted me to hole up in an apartment they use for people under protective custody. It took a lot of yelling and screaming before I convinced them that I had to be free."

"Ann, are you sure that's smart?" Nancy asked.

"It may not be smart, but it's the only way I'll be able to help your father out of this mess. After all, it's my fault he's in it. By the way, I'm sorry about the judge. He didn't deserve that."

"No, he really didn't." Nancy was beginning to like Ann more and more. Ann was, in effect, risking her life to help Carson Drew. And it was very generous of her to express sympathy for Jonathan Renk.

"I'm also sorry the trip to the Grand didn't pan out. Did you wait for the guy long?"

Nancy had stretched the truth the day before. She simply told Ann her source hadn't shown. Evidently that part of the story had not made the news. Perhaps they hadn't believed her. But Ann Granger would, and now that Ann was out of the hospital Nancy knew she would want the truth. She told Ann all about her harrowing half-hour in the kidnap car.

Ann was horrified. "Nancy, I'm sorry! First I get Carson into trouble, and now you. I had no idea—"

"I know you didn't," Nancy assured her. "Now, maybe you should change your mind about protective custody. It was you they were after."

On the other end of the line, the reporter was very quiet. Finally, she cleared her throat. "No. I can't. Don't get me wrong, Nancy. I'm not all that brave. But I have a family tradition to uphold," Ann said. "My parents risked their lives in the early sixties, marching for their civil rights. Now it's my turn to risk mine to protect my First Amendment rights. End of speech. What can I do to help?"

Nancy and Ned had discussed this the night before, so Nancy was ready with an answer. "We need to know if Mid-City was the only scam those guys were running. Can you find out what else its parent corporation owns? They're hiding something more, and we've got to find out what."

"I'll try. That's all I can do."

"Great. Since you don't have a car, I'll have Bess pick you up, okay?"

"That's too risky," Ann said. "Hanging out with me will put her in danger."

"She'll understand. I'll phone her, then you can call her and let her know when you'll be ready."

"Will do. Luck to us. 'Bye."

Nancy hung up. She knew they'd need more than luck to get through this. Then she made a quick call to Bess, who agreed to drive Ann wherever she needed to go.

Nancy ducked into the shower. Afterward she pulled a navy suit and a pale blue blouse from the closet. A single strand of pearls and her navy blue heels completed the ensemble.

Nancy considered this her "working woman" outfit. She wore it whenever she had to invade the nine-to-five world. For a few hours that day, she would be invading her father's.

Ned called just as she was leaving. "Man Friday reporting in," he said. "I've got George's car. I figured I'd start with the cable company."

59

"And tell them what?"

"I'm an insurance investigator trying to track a white van involved in a hit-and-run accident. They'll swear it wasn't one of theirs. Then they should give me a couple of leads to other companies that use white vans. And so on and so on."

"Ned, that's brilliant!"

"I thought so, too. Meet you for lunch at the Pizza Palace. One o'clock. I'll tell Ann and Bess, too. That way if one of us doesn't show up, we'll know that person's in trouble. Good luck."

Luck seemed to be on everyone's mind that day, Nancy thought as she locked the door behind her.

The law offices of Carson Drew and his associates always made Nancy feel as if she should whisper. With its solid mahogany desks, leather-upholstered chairs, and wood-paneled walls, there was a quiet, dignified aura about it. The tang of lemon oil scented the air, mixed with the smell of leather-bound law books.

Her father's secretary, Ms. Hanson, welcomed Nancy and opened the door of Carson Drew's office for her. "If there's anything you need—if you have any questions—just ask. We'll help in any way we can." She slipped silently from the room.

Her back against the door, Nancy looked around. There were so many places a bug might be hidden—behind any of the hundreds of books that lined one wall, in the lamps or ceiling fixtures, under the furniture.

But she decided to eliminate the obvious first. Crossing to her father's enormous desk, Nancy opened the top righthand drawer and removed a wooden box, a container for cassette tapes.

"I will only tape a client's conversation with his permission," her father had explained. "And only for important information that I need to remember word for word. It's treated completely confidentially. When I'm not there, that box is locked."

Nancy used the key Carson had given her and lifted the lid. There were slots for twenty-four cassettes, and all the slots were filled, just as her father had told her they would be.

But she wasn't ready to accept that at face value. Someone might have removed a tape and replaced it with another to make sure the first one wouldn't be missed.

She played them all on fast forward so that she could be certain those two dozen tapes were what they were supposed to be. They were.

That done, she began a thorough search of the office. There wasn't much on her father's desk: a blotter; the telephone; a pen set in an oiled walnut holder; a paperweight, a heavy glass dome with a black-eyed susan embedded in it. A ladybug was perched at the edge of one leaf, and the top of the dome had holes for pencils. Nancy pulled off her jacket, draped it over a chair, and went to work.

An hour later she sat down, discouraged and frustrated. She had been completely sure that either someone had swiped one of her dad's tapes or that they had bugged his office and recorded his voice that way. But after going over his office with a fine-tooth comb, she hadn't found a thing. Where was that luck everyone had wished her that morning?

At the sound of voices, Nancy looked up. There was a courier from a messenger service in the outer office, drinking coffee from a Styrofoam cup while Ms. Hanson prepared an envelope for him to take. From their conversation, Nancy could tell he was a regular visitor. Nancy waited impatiently in her father's office until he finally left. Now she could check for bugs out there.

Ms. Hanson sat at her desk, her face taut with anxiety as Nancy examined the outer office. It took longer because there were filing cabinets to check, but in the end the result was the same —no bug.

"I've had it," Nancy said finally. "I can't find a bug." She retrieved her jacket and tucked her purse under her arm. "Thanks for putting up with me," she told the secretary.

"I'm almost sorry there was nothing here,"

Ms. Hanson said. "It's just so awful. If you think of any way that I can help, please call me."

Nancy promised she would and said goodbye. As she walked through the halls, she was surprised at the amount of traffic in and out of the office—mail clerks, maintenance workers, couriers, clients. Any one of them could have slipped into her father's office and—

And what? she asked herself. Would she be able to find out in time? For that matter, how much time did she have? Her father was sure he'd have a pretrial date by the end of the day. Then she'd know.

Her second chore for the day took Nancy to several different locations. Her goal was to learn whatever she could about the Gold Star Cab Company. Each place she went, she told them the same story.

"Hi. I'm a student at Emerson College. I'm writing a term paper on the growth of transportation in River Heights. I've researched the bus service. Can you help me with the cab companies?"

She always followed the question with a winning smile. It never failed to make things easier. Everyone she talked to was very cooperative, some telling her far more than she'd ever need to know.

After visits to the Office of Public Safety, the

central headquarters of the River Heights Police Department, and the Hacks Bureau, Nancy was beginning to wonder if she was on the right track. There seemed to be nothing unusual about the Gold Star Cab Company.

Checking her watch, Nancy left the building that housed the Hacks Bureau. Unless she hurried, she'd be late for her lunch meeting with Ned, Bess, and Ann.

Nancy tucked her notes in her bag and started across the street to the lot where she had left her car.

She heard trouble coming before she could see it. It was the sound of a powerful engine being pushed to its maximum. Seconds later she saw it—a dark late-model car racing around the corner and heading directly for her at top speed!

Chapter

Nine

STILL SHAKEN BY her near encounter with the dark car, Nancy met Ned at the door of the Pizza Palace just as he was leaving to go look for her. "There you are. We've already ordered."

Ann and Bess were waiting in a booth, Bess's deep pink jumpsuit clashing with the bright orange and purple vinyl seats. The place was jammed with students from a nearby junior college.

"Stop staring at me," Nancy ordered her friends. "I got dirty dodging a car that tried to hit me. He missed me by a hair."

"A drunk driver?" Ann asked.

"Not on your life—I mean, my life. He tried his best to hit me."

Ned's expression was grim. "Did you get his license number?"

"No. I jumped back behind a filthy minivan at the curb. By the time I could look, the car was gone and I was dirty. Did you guys have any trouble today?"

"Not a bit," Bess answered. "It's been fun."

Ann chuckled. "It's a good thing she was with me. One Bess Marvin smile, and every male in the computer room is searching data banks to get the information you asked for."

"That's great. Keep smiling, Bess." Nancy turned to Ned. "How'd you do?"

He removed a notepad from his pocket. "So far I've got the names of seven businesses that use white vans. I'll keep at it this afternoon. Then tomorrow I'll hit all these places and see if I can find your van with the bent fender. How'd things go at the office?"

Before Nancy could respond, a waitress slid two huge pizzas onto the table. They smelled incredibly good, and Nancy's stomach growled in anticipation.

"I didn't find a thing in my dad's office," she said, removing her first slice. "Whoever planted the bug must have come back and taken it out. As for the cab company, that was a washout, too."

"What's a cab company got to do with anything?" Ann asked.

Nancy explained about the voice she'd heard over the two-way radio in her abductor's car and in the Gold Star cab. "Gold Star checked out okay," she said. "In business over twenty years, owned by two local men. They have ten cabs and a dynamite safety record. Not a single accident in the past three years."

Ann peeled off a circle of pepperoni from her slice. "I could have told you that. It was one of the businesses insured by—" She paused, frowning. "By Mid-City Insurance Company," she said slowly.

"Coincidence?" Ned asked, gazing at Nancy.

"I don't know. On paper they're certainly good guys," she responded. "Several public service awards, one of them from the Gray Panthers for offering senior citizens lower fares."

Ann chewed the sliver of pepperoni thoughtfully. "You know, losing their insurance company must have been devastating, especially to a small business like Gold Star. It would be interesting to know what it took for them to recover."

"So that's how an idea for an article is born," Bess said. "Somehow I thought it would be more—exciting."

Nancy didn't really pay much attention to the conversation as they finished their pizzas. That dispatcher's voice—she was so sure it had been the same man on the radio of both cars!

And there was something else nagging at the back of her mind, a tiny bell warning her that she had missed something. But what could it be?

Ann and Bess finished their pizza and began digging for their money.

"We've got to get back to the *Record,*" Ann

explained. "The computer guys are waiting for us. Where are you going now, Nancy?"

"I'm not sure. Maybe back to my dad's office."

"Don't give up," Bess said, slipping into her jacket. "We're close to an answer. I'm sure of it."

"I wish I could be as sure," Nancy said, after Ann and Bess had left. "Something's bugging me, something I've overlooked, but I can't put my finger on it."

"Finish your pizza," Ned suggested. "And stop thinking about it. It'll come. In the meantime, I'll order another slice. I'm still hungry."

"Take mine." Nancy slid hers over to him. Her appetite had vanished.

They sat and talked for quite a while after Ned had finished. Having lunch together was an occasion that happened so rarely that they wanted to draw it out.

Finally Ned collected the money from the table and went to pay the cashier. While he was gone, Nancy took one last look at the notes she had made, trying to pinpoint the reason for her uneasiness. At last she saw it!

She left the booth and met Ned just as he was pocketing his receipt. "What do you think of this? Ann said that someone had left a tip for her to see a woman out at Crimson Oaks. Then she got the court order and never followed up on it."

"So?"

"One of the public service awards Gold Star received was from the Crimson Oaks Village

Association. I know it isn't much, but shouldn't I check it out?"

"Let's make that 'we.' You call Ann and get the woman's name while I go get George's car. I'll meet you out front."

The name was Vera Harvey, and she lived in building four of Crimson Oaks' five highrises. And as Ned and Nancy approached the building, they saw a Gold Star cab pulling away with a passenger in the back. Nancy wasn't sure whether it was an omen or not.

The building's doorman looked them over with friendly curiosity. "Mrs. Harvey? I don't think she's in."

The lobby was very comfortable, filled with easy chairs and palms. Several elderly residents sat there, chatting and reading. The doorman called to one of them. "Have you seen Mrs. Harvey come back yet?"

One woman shook her head. "It's too early. Her physical therapy lasts until four."

"Oh, yes. I forgot." The doorman thanked her and turned back to them. "It might be better if you came back tomorrow. She usually doesn't feel too good until the day after her therapy."

"Has she been sick?" Nancy asked.

"She's had a time of it. Got hurt in an accident last year. Her own fault—too proud to ask someone for a ride. Insisted on taking a cab instead. She knew it wasn't safe."

"Taking a cab?" Ned asked.

"Taking a Gold Star cab sure isn't. That phone on my desk is a direct line to the place, but nobody uses it unless they're desperate."

"Just a minute," Nancy spoke calmly, hiding her excitement. "Mrs. Harvey was hurt in a Gold Star cab last year?"

"Hurt isn't the word. We almost lost her. Only good thing about that cab company is that they took good care of her."

"You mean their insurance company?" Nancy asked, wanting to be certain she understood clearly.

"Not the way we hear it. You should talk to Tom Tyler, but I saw him drive past awhile ago. Gold Star's owners hired a fancy ambulance to move her from County General up to Pinebrook."

Ned's brows shot up. "The private hospital an hour away from here?"

"That's the one. The place where rich folks go when they're sick. Gold Star paid all the bills —and, mind you, she was there two months. They're even footing the bill for the physical therapy."

"That was very generous of them," Nancy said.

"Smart is what it was. It was their fault. The cab's brakes failed. If she'd made a stink, somebody would have gone to jail over the condition of that cab."

"Poor?" Ned asked.

"Rattletraps, pure and simple. Falling apart. Three other people in this building have been in one when it's had an accident. They weren't hurt, just shaken up. But, as I said, we don't ride with Gold Star unless we're desperate."

"Let's go, Ned," Nancy said, pulling him toward the door. "Thank you," she told the doorman. "We'll try to come back tomorrow."

"You look as if you're about to explode," Ned said outside on the sidewalk.

"I am! It's a big break, if I can just figure out how this all fits in to what's happened to my dad."

"Why's it such a big break?"

"Because what we heard in there does *not* jibe with what I was told this morning. The doorman mentioned four accidents, one of them serious. Those accidents aren't on record down at central headquarters."

"How couldn't they be? Especially Mrs. Harvey's."

"I don't know. But even more important than that is that Gold Star had to know Mid-City was a scam!"

They'd reached George's car and were talking across the hood. "You're right," Ned said. "They would have expected their insurance company to take care of their bills."

"Exactly. And the doorman was very clear. Gold Star paid Mrs. Harvey's bills, *not* Gold Star's insurer. They had to have filed a claim with Mid-City, but nothing would have happened because Mid-City didn't exist," Nancy said. "So why didn't they report that to the police? Why didn't they scream bloody murder?"

"Because they knew about Mid-City from the beginning, that's why," Ann said half an hour later, slamming a computer printout onto her kitchen table.

"How?" Ned asked.

The reporter's eyes blazed with fury. "There are fourteen men on the board of directors of the corporation that was listed as Mid-City's parent company. You with me so far?"

Nancy nodded.

"Three of those men listed themselves as owners of Mid-City, and two will probably go to jail," Ann said. "That leaves eleven others on that board of directors. Two of those eleven own the Gold Star Cab Company."

"So they were all in it together," Bess chimed in. "That's what they were trying to hide!"

"Is it?" Nancy asked. She was troubled. It was too simple. "I wonder. It could be a case of one hand not knowing what the other was doing."

"That's possible," Ann admitted. "A board of directors isn't usually a close-knit group. They don't have meetings that often."

"In some corporations, only once a year," Ned said. "So the Gold Star guys could say that they had no idea their fellow directors from the parent company were running Mid-City Insurance. If they were smart enough, no one would be able to prove otherwise."

"They're probably smart enough, all right," Nancy grumbled. "They've got to be hiding something else. But what?"

"It's an interesting question," her father said when Nancy and Ned filled him in that evening. "Think you can find the answer in five days?"

Nancy's mouth dropped open. "They've set your pretrial for five days from now?"

"That's really rushing things, isn't it?" Ned asked.

"Indeed it is," Carson Drew said. "But in comparison to the next item I have to tell you, the pretrial date is the good news."

Nancy steeled herself. "What's happened, Dad?"

"The police found an envelope with ten thousand dollars in cash in Jonathan's office safe."

"And?" Nancy said, feeling a sudden chill.

"My prints were all over it. And the envelope had been addressed to Jonathan on one of our office typewriters. I might as well slap a label on my forehead and mail myself off to prison."

Chapter

Ten

N ANCY ROLLED OUT of bed the next morning. Her eyelids felt gritty, and her head ached. Time was against her, and she couldn't decide what to do. She only had part of the day free. The memorial service for Jonathan Renk was that afternoon, and she wanted to attend.

She wondered if she should go back to her father's office that morning to try to figure out how this last stunt had been accomplished. The stationery was kept in Ms. Hanson's office. Her father had told her and Ned that he would have no reason to handle an envelope at all.

"Ms. Hanson types the letters and brings them to me to sign," he told her. "I never even *see* the envelopes. I don't remember handling a blank one they could type a name on."

It was a puzzle, to say the least, but Nancy finally decided that visiting the office again that day would be a waste of time. Instead, she'd go to Gold Star. The truth had to be there.

Ned had protested that it was much too dangerous. And Nancy did agree with him, but she also felt she had no other choice. With the pretrial date right around the corner, she had to go with what she had. And what she had was the Gold Star Cab Company.

The girl who walked into the garage of Gold Star Cab an hour and a half later had a mop of short, mahogany-brown curls and enormous round glasses. She was chewing gum as if she hadn't eaten in a week, and the outfit she wore —an oversize top and baggy jeans—disguised her slender figure.

Even Bess and George wouldn't recognize me, Nancy told herself, making her gum sound off in a series of firecracker *pop-pop-pops*. It was a part of her new character. She was about to do the acting job of her life.

Gold Star used half of the street-level space of a five-story parking garage, and a business called Fleet's had the other half. The garage had been built with two entrances, one on McConnell Street and the other on the street behind, Bennett Avenue. The cab company and Fleet's used the entrance on McConnell, so after Nancy left her Mustang on the third level of the public garage, she had to walk around the block to get to Gold Star.

Just inside the door was the dispatcher's office. Nancy ambled into it, eyeing the stocky red-headed man who was bellowing at a cabbie over a two-way radio. The voice was the same one she had heard when she was on the floor of that car.

I'm definitely in the right place, she thought. While she waited for the dispatcher to finish, she examined the cabs parked along the walls on the side.

Four were old, dented, and rusty. The rest— she counted thirteen before the man finished —were late models, clean, bright, and shiny, and their gold paint glistened under the fluorescent lights. There were more cabs, but only the front half of the space was lit, so she couldn't see the ones along the rear wall.

Here was another interesting mystery. According to the Hacks Bureau, Gold Star was a small business with only ten cars in its fleet.

"Need a cab?" the man asked, and Nancy turned around.

"Huh-uh," she said with a saucy smile. "A job. I've worked as a dispatcher since I was sixteen. Want references?"

"No. Don't want another dispatcher, either."

Nancy arranged her face in an expression of deep disappointment. "Hey, you aren't going to cry, are you?" He jammed a long, fat cigar into his mouth. "It won't get you a job as a dispatcher, but smile and you may get a job as a cabbie. How old are you, anyway?"

"Eighteen." Nancy looked hopeful—she hoped.

"Got a driver's license?"

"Sure, but it takes time and money to get a hack license and I need the job *now*."

The man winked. "We'll take care of that for you." Then he began testing her familiarity with River Heights and its surrounding areas. Nancy knew her hometown like the back of her hand. When he had finished questioning her, she knew he was impressed.

He ran a wooden match along the surface of his battered desk and lit the cigar. A cloud of foul yellow smoke drifted around his head. "What's your name?"

"Nancy Nickerson. Here's my ID." She began rooting in her bag, made from a pair of old jeans. She removed a large yellow comb and put it on his desk. Then came a tube of lipstick, a paperback book, half a sandwich, a two-way mirror, and a candy bar. "It's in here somewhere."

"Never mind. Nancy Nickerson," he mumbled, writing it down. "My name's Brownley. I'm the boss."

They were suddenly interrupted by a deep, male voice calling for him. "Mr. Brownley?"

"What is it, Dayton?" A good-looking, young blond cabbie appeared in the doorway—the same one who had picked up Nancy two days before.

"My lunch is over, and I'm going back out. Which car should I take?" Dayton looked over at Nancy. She could tell he was trying to decide if they'd ever met.

"Take the one you used earlier," Brownley answered.

"Okay, see you later."

Brownley grunted, "So long," and then turned back to Nancy.

"We've got to get your picture taken. Follow me."

Heaving himself from a swivel chair that creaked loudly, he led her into a storage closet behind the office and stood her against a white wall. Taking a Polaroid camera off a shelf, he said, "Smile." Before she could do it, the flash went off in her eyes.

"Okay. You start tomorrow, eight to four."

That was a problem. It would be harder to poke around in broad daylight. "Uh, couldn't I work at night? I take a couple of classes during the day. I could even start this evening."

"We don't need night drivers."

It took five minutes of haggling before Brownley agreed to let her work from four to midnight.

"Gee, thanks," she said, popping her gum. She looked out the window of his office at the cabs. "Any of those have stick shifts? What kind ya got, anyway?" She was out into the garage, trotting past the lines of cars before Brownley could get through his office door.

He followed, panting. "Hey! You'll be using one up front. I choose, you don't."

Nancy had already walked half the length of the space and from there could see all the cabs and the vehicles she had not been able to make out before.

"Oh. Okay," she said and strolled back toward him. "See ya tonight. Thanks again." And she ducked under the rollup door.

Nancy congratulated herself on an Oscar-winning performance, especially the last sixty seconds of it. It had been very difficult to hide how excited she was after she had seen the vehicles at the rear of the garage.

Parked in the left corner, almost invisible in the gloom, was a dirty white van, with strips of tape over the lettering on its sides—and a bent right fender.

Chapter

Eleven

JUDGE JONATHAN RENK'S memorial was well-attended. The church was filled with the most respected members of the community and a few nationally known political figures.

The media was barred from the service itself. Ann, feeling awkward about attending, had decided not to come. But it looked as if every other reporter in the Midwest was standing outside the church, waiting to pounce on key figures as they left. The Drews, Bess, and Ned avoided them by leaving through a rear door.

They all went back to the judge's house with the housekeeper. "It was lovely, wasn't it?" Mrs. O'Hara kept asking Nancy, her father, and Ned. Bess had gone into the living room.

"It went very well," Nancy said, helping her

remove her coat and hanging it in the closet off the kitchen. The house was filling up with people who had come to pay their respects. "I guess the guests are starting to arrive. Hannah and Bess will help you keep things running smoothly."

Mrs. O'Hara dabbed at her eyes. "It's so sad. But he hadn't been the same since before Miss Martha died. You could tell that, couldn't you, Mr. Drew?"

"Well, I hadn't seen him that often, Katherine. Once he dropped out of our weekly card games, I—"

The housekeeper's eyes widened, and she stared at Nancy's father. "He dropped out? When?"

"It's been almost a year. We assumed he'd just lost the heart for it."

Mrs. O'Hara looked away, a bewildered expression on her face. "Then where was he going?"

"Pardon?"

"Mr. Drew, the judge left here every Wednesday night, the way he's always done since I came to work here."

"He wasn't with us. Perhaps he found a new group. They never played here?"

"No, sir, always somewhere else. Sometimes he drove, sometimes someone came to pick him up. Last summer, it was, he was going two and three times a week."

"Perhaps he was going somewhere else," Nancy suggested. "I mean, to the theater or something."

"No, lass. He had a routine. Whenever he was going to play cards, he'd sit at his desk and practice shuffling and dealing. That's how I could tell."

Carson Drew smiled sadly. "He always joked that if he hadn't gone into law, he'd have been a dealer in Las Vegas."

"Aye. He and Miss Martha, they were a pair. All the time she was sick, he'd go to Pinebrook to see her with a deck of cards in his pocket. They'd enjoy a game together there in her hospital room until she couldn't play any longer. I—I had no idea he wasn't playing with you anymore, Mr. Carson."

Nancy's eyes locked with those of Ned, who had been listening quietly. "Pinebrook?" she asked.

"Yes. He wanted the best for her. A lovely place."

Mrs. O'Hara launched into a lengthy description of the hospital. Nancy, knowing that her father was enough of a captive audience, excused herself and Ned, and they slipped into the library. Closing the door, they crossed to the judge's desk.

The fingerprinting dust was gone, and the window had been repaired. But Jonathan Renk's presence remained.

Trial By Fire

"What are you going to do?" Ned asked.

Nancy picked up the phone. "Call Ann. We may have found another link." She dialed Ann's number at the newspaper.

"Where are you?" the reporter asked.

"At my uncle Jon's. Got a task for you. Can you find out the dates that Mrs. Harvey was a patient at Pinebrook?"

"I don't see why not. What's up?"

"My uncle Jon's wife was a patient there over a year ago. Mrs. Harvey was there for two months. I'm just wondering if they were there at the same time."

"Now, that would be interesting, wouldn't it? Give me your number. I'll get back to you as soon as I can."

Nancy looked around the library as she replaced the phone. She had planned to ask Mrs. O'Hara if she could check the judge's files the next day, but since she wasn't here—

She opened the desk drawers.

"What are you looking for?" Ned asked.

"I don't know," Nancy admitted. "Anything that'll help explain why my uncle would agree to help frame my dad."

"In other words, what had the judge done that could be used against him as blackmail."

Nancy looked over at the wall of photographs, all with the judge's smiling face, and sighed. "I guess so."

Ned cupped her chin in his hand. "He was

83

very special to you, wasn't he? I'm sorry. I thought he was just your father's friend." He held her for a minute, smoothing her hair. "You must hate having to poke through his things."

Nancy nodded and wrapped her arms around his waist. "I do. But I have to. Four days, Ned! I'm so worried that I won't have worked this out by then and my father will be bound over for trial. The sooner this is cleared up, the faster people will forget, and then he can resume his practice."

After he brushed his lips across hers, Ned gently pushed her away. "Then you'd better get to work, huh?"

She smiled. "I'd better get to work." She went back to the desk.

The only items of interest were the judge's checkbook and a box of canceled checks. Nothing unusual there—payments to the phone, gas, and power companies.

The lower drawer was filled with file folders. Nancy sat on the floor and flipped through the labels. Under "Deeds" she found the one for the house and the Renks' vacation home at a nearby lake. There were also several papers clipped to each deed. They were from a bank.

"Ned, look at these."

He left the drawer of the file cabinet he was going through. After a moment he said, "Judge Renk borrowed money from two different banks and used this house and his cottage as collateral."

"Perhaps to pay my aunt Martha's medical bills," Nancy said.

"I'm not so sure," he said slowly. "I saw several file folders in the cabinet with names of banks on the labels. They're loan agreements, too. I'll pull them. See if there are any more in his desk."

There weren't. Ned had found the only items of interest. They sat on the floor again and spread the folders out around them.

"This is incredible," Ned said. "In this past year, Judge Renk borrowed over a hundred thousand dollars!"

"And paid it all back with interest—when? One bank a month for the past six months."

"Where'd he get the money?" Ned asked. He raised an eyebrow. "He couldn't have been that good at cards, could he?"

"You'll have to ask my dad. Look, before we jump to conclusions, let's check the dates on any canceled checks made out to Pinebrook. See if they match up with the dates he got the loans."

They searched through several boxes of canceled checks. Jonathan Renk had paid the balance due on his wife's hospital bill two months after her death. Thirty-nine thousand dollars.

"So why the loans for the hundred thousand?" Nancy muttered to herself. She bundled the folders together and put them aside to show her father.

Ned had begun looking at the photographs on the wall. "He sure had some high-powered friends," Ned commented. There were pictures of the judge with presidents, senators, a governor, and nationally known mayors of large cities.

Nancy had joined Ned to look at the photographs. "That's my aunt Martha. It must have been taken at Pinebrook."

Martha Renk, wearing a robe and looking thinner than Nancy remembered, sat at a table with her husband and two nurses. Each had cards in their hands and smiles on their faces. But the face that caught Nancy's attention was in the background. She gasped.

"What is it?"

"Ned! That looks like the man who tried to kidnap me!"

"Which one?"

There were six people standing behind the four at the card table. Nancy pointed to the man on the end. She had only seen his features for a few seconds, but thought she remembered his thin face, light eyes, and narrow lips.

Someone knocked on the door. Ned opened it, and Bess peered in. "Oh, there you are. Ned, we need some help with a fifty-pound bag of ice."

"Sure. I'll be back as soon as I can," he told Nancy.

Nancy turned back to the photograph. She had to be sure it was the same man.

Taking it to the desk, she removed it from its frame. Without the glare of the glass, the face was clearer. It definitely was he. The judge had written the names of the people in the photo on the back. Philip Reston. That's what the dispatcher had called him! Res, not Wes! She had seen the name before, too. Where?

The phone rang, and Nancy snatched the receiver to her ear. "Renk residence."

"It's Ann, Nancy. They were there at the same time, but Mrs. Harvey wouldn't tell me a thing. In fact, she sounded terrified. She hung up on me. I asked a doctor friend to find out for me."

"He called Pinebrook?"

"Yes. Mrs. Harvey was there five weeks before Mrs. Renk died, and she went home three weeks afterward."

"And I just found a photo," Nancy said, "of my uncle Jon and a nasty character named Philip Reston, the man who snatched me out of the Grand." She slapped her forehead. "*Now* I remember where I've seen the name! He's one of the owners of Gold Star!"

Ann said, "Uh-oh. This is getting better and better, and worse and worse. Nancy, you'd better stay away from that place."

"I can't! Now that we've established a link between Reston and my uncle? No way! We're coming down the pike, Ann, I'm sure of it."

Ann snorted. "If you aren't careful, the pike will be coming down on you."

When Nancy arrived at Gold Star late that afternoon, Brownley handed her a hack's license that looked perfectly legitimate. "Don't advertise how you got this," he said, warning her. "That wouldn't be smart."

"Okay by me," Nancy said, popping gum at top speed.

"Take one-six-one," he said. "Don't hit any bumps or you'll bash your head in. It needs shocks. And if you get it dirty, run it through the car wash next door on your way back in. See you at midnight."

"Is the car wash open at night? That seems odd."

"Yeah, well, they just keep a skeleton crew on. Must make money or they wouldn't do it."

"Do *you* work twenty-four hours a day?" Nancy then asked, needing to know when she could search his office. "When do you eat?"

"My, my, aren't we full of questions. What's it to you when I work?"

"I thought if I was close by, I could bring you a pizza or something. I didn't mean to bother you, just wanted to help."

He grinned. "You're an okay kid. Nobody ever offered before. I have dinner around ten, but don't make a special trip if you've got a fare."

As Nancy walked through the garage to her

assigned car, she saw Jim Dayton getting out of his cab.

"Hi," he called to her. "Working the evening shift, huh? Tough break."

"Well, not exactly." Nancy stopped, and then said, "I asked for it. I need to make some extra money fast."

"I know what you mean. I'm in between semesters from college now, and I'm doing this to pick up some fast cash myself," he said. "Oh, my name's Jim Dayton."

"Nancy Nickerson. Nice to meet you."

"Same here. They don't have too many female drivers around here, you know."

Nancy quickly glanced at her watch. "And they'll have one less if I don't get out of here," she said smiling. "I'll be seeing you around."

"I hope so," Jim answered. Nancy noticed that his incredibly blue eyes sparkled even in the harsh light of the garage.

Nancy got into the car and started the engine. Too bad this guy's only temporary, she thought. He's friendly, and he might know something.

By ten o'clock Nancy had driven over two hundred miles. Her money bag was full, her back was stiff, and her rear end was numb from sitting. But if Brownley was away from his desk, she wouldn't be sitting much longer.

Turning onto McConnell, she made a pass by the garage to see if the office was empty. It was.

Unfortunately, Brownley was standing just outside of it talking to a tall, thin man, who turned just then and glanced out into the street.

"Oh, no!" Nancy whispered.

It was Philip Reston. If he got a close look at her, her life wouldn't be worth a ten-cent tip.

Chapter

Twelve

NANCY EASED PAST the garage so the sound of the motor wouldn't attract the attention of either man. What should she do? She wasn't sure whether Brownley had seen her.

Grabbing the mike, she called in. After a second, Brownley answered. "Hey, kid, did you just pass here?"

"Sure, on the way to twenty-five-twelve Bennett. Is something wrong with the radio? I called you three times before you answered."

"Guess I didn't hear you," he said. "I was talking to somebody."

"Oh. Sorry. Want me to call back?"

"No, I'm finished." Just what Nancy wanted to hear. "Why don't you knock off early? Call it a night. Come on in when you've finished this run. Nothing's happening tonight."

"Will do. One-six-one out."

She drove a couple of blocks farther and parked long enough to put in the money her imaginary fare would have paid. Then she doubled back, edging around the corner onto Mc-Connell again. Reston was standing by a late-model Buick parked on the street just beyond the garage. It was a dead ringer for the car that had tried to run her over the day before.

To kill more time, Nancy ran the cab through the car wash next door, sitting in the vehicle as it glided through the cycles. It seemed to take much too short a time. Reston was still out front, but she couldn't put off going in any longer.

The Gold Star sign—a brightly lit rectangle above the broad rollup door—spilled its gaudy light into the cab as she drove under it. From the corner of her eye, Nancy saw Reston staring at her with a puzzled expression.

After a moment's hesitation, he got in the Buick and started the engine. Nancy's hand shook slightly as she opened the cab door. But Reston was gone. She'd survived her first shift as a Gold Star cabbie.

"Not bad, Nickerson," Brownley said, counting her money. "Lay off that gum, and you'll do even better."

"I'll think about it." Nancy removed the cushion she'd brought from the front seat of the cab. "Where can I leave this?"

He nodded toward a bank of lockers just beyond his office. "Snag one for yourself. You have to supply your own lock, though."

Nancy walked along the row of lockers, hoping for an empty one as close to the back of the garage as possible. The second and third from the end were available.

She crammed the cushion into one and hunted for a pen to scratch "Ellison" off the strip of adhesive tape that served as the name tag on the locker door. After squeezing "Nickerson" on it, she glanced at the names on either side —Eastman, which had a monster combination lock on the door, and Tyler, with no lock at all.

Nancy stared at it. "T. Tyler." The doorman at Mrs. Harvey's building had mentioned a Tyler. The same man? she wondered.

"Hey, Nickerson! Find an empty?" Brownley shouted from the office.

"Uh—yes." Nancy slammed the door closed and ambled toward the front. Perhaps the next night she'd be able to slip away from her locker and see what else was back there in the dark.

One thing she *had* been able to see. The white van was gone.

"I don't understand why you wanted me to come with you," Ann said as the elevator in Crimson Oaks building two rose to the tenth floor.

93

"According to the doorman in building four, this Mr. Tyler knows your Mrs. Harvey and knows all about the accident. He may be able to convince Mrs. Harvey to talk to us."

Ann looked doubtful. "As frightened as she sounded on the phone, it would take a subpoena to make her open up."

"Even that might not work," Nancy said, smiling at her. "It hasn't worked with you."

The elderly man who answered their knock eyed them with curiosity. He had sandy hair and laugh lines that made his face look permanently happy. "Which one of you did I talk to this morning?" he asked.

"That was me," Nancy said. "Thank you for seeing us. I'm Nancy Nickerson, and this is Ann Granger."

"Delighted," he said. "Thomas Tyler at your service."

Nancy glanced around the neat, comfortable apartment. The top of a corner table was cluttered with framed photographs, probably of his family. She walked over to it and noticed a picture of—Jim Dayton!

What was his photo doing here? She decided she'd work in the question during the course of the conversation.

"Please," Mr. Tyler said. "Have a seat." He seemed determined to be the perfect host. Charming and witty, he had them laughing over

94

cups of tea for half an hour before they got around to the subject they had come to discuss.

"Mr. Tyler," Nancy said, beginning, "did you work for the Gold Star Cab Company?"

"I was their mechanic from the first day they hit the streets until a year and a half ago, when they kicked me out. Said I should retire, and saw that I did."

"Brownley and Reston?"

"That's right. First they brought in a new man—to help me, they said—a thug who didn't know a brake shoe from a bedroom slipper. Then they cut back on my hours, but they still paid me for full-time. The new man didn't do a thing, which took care of the rolling stock. Everything began to fall apart."

"That doesn't make sense," Ann said.

"No, it doesn't. Then they closed off the lower level where I was doing the maintenance work."

Nancy held up a hand. "The street level isn't the lowest level?"

"No, indeed. There's a basement. The entrance was at the back on the right. You just drove on down. They put a door in there to close it up, and then they locked it. It cut the amount of our parking spaces in half, because I then had to work on the street level."

"Why did they do that?" Nancy asked.

"I still don't know. They fired drivers who'd been with them for years and began taking on part-timers. Then they bought new cabs, but they never used them."

"It sounds as if they wanted to lose money," Ann said.

"Well, they didn't, even though the old cabs began to fall apart. You know riding in a Gold Star cab has become hazardous to your health. I even told my grandson that before he started working there."

"Your grandson? After all you went through, why would he want to work there?" Nancy asked, now knowing Jim's connection to Mr. Tyler.

"All Jim would say was that good-paying temp jobs are hard to come by. I know it's only going to be a few weeks, but I still wish he hadn't taken it."

Nancy thought that sounded familiar. Ned was in the same predicament, only he hadn't found a job.

A sudden suspicion began to grow in Nancy's mind. "Were you working for Gold Star when Mrs. Harvey was hurt?"

"No, that happened a couple of months after they put me out to pasture. But of course I heard about it. Crimson Oaks is like a small town. And I felt real bad about what happened to Vera. Haven't had a decent night's sleep since."

"Why?" Ann asked.

"That cab's brakes had failed twice before I left Gold Star. I warned Brownley that they needed work. But they didn't do a thing, Ms.

Granger. Not before I left, and not after, because I saw that cab on the street."

"You did all you could," Nancy said.

"No. I could have reported them. If I had, Vera Harvey wouldn't be walking with a cane today."

Now Nancy was sure her suspicion was right. "Mr. Tyler, you're Ann Granger's source, aren't you?" she asked.

"*What?*" Ann asked.

Mr. Tyler turned pink. "Young lady, you're too smart for your own good. But so am I. You're that lawyer's daughter, aren't you? You were on the news. They said that you're a detective."

The reporter stood up. "You mean, she's right?"

"She's right. I'm sorry, Ms. Granger. It never occurred to me I'd get you and Mr. Drew in so much trouble. Believe me, I'd never have let them put you in jail. I'd have come forward. Still plan to. You just tell me when."

Ann leaned over and shook his hand. "Mr. Tyler, it means a great deal to me to hear you say that, but I don't want you to do it. There's a principle involved here. I'm protected by the First Amendment, and I intend to stick by my guns."

"Well, let me know if you change your mind," he said.

Nancy noticed that Ann didn't mention that the members of the grand jury weren't the only people who wanted to know his name.

"As I said, I'm sorry about the trouble I caused," Mr. Tyler went on. "I just couldn't sit back and see anyone else hurt, so I called you."

"But why the newspaper?"

"After Vera's accident, I went to Brownley and Reston and told them if they didn't do something about those cabs, I'd report them to the Hacks Bureau. I thought Reston would beat me up, he was so mad, but Brownley cooled him down. Said I was right and they'd take care of things."

"But they didn't," Ann said.

"No, but I didn't find out until recently. My daughter in New York City had been nagging me to go and live with her. Well, I tried it for almost a year, but that was enough. Too many people on that island. I moved back here and found the same old cabs in the same rotten condition. My grandson told me it's a miracle one car lasts for an entire shift."

"When did you move back here, Mr. Tyler?" Nancy asked.

"A couple of months back. I went to the Hacks Bureau, and they sent me over to Public Safety. I explained that I wanted to report Gold Star, and they sent me somewhere else. Took me awhile before I realized I was getting the runaround. Everybody seemed to be covering for Gold Star."

Nancy thought back to the glowing reports she had gotten about Gold Star cabs from those very same offices, and wondered what she had stumbled onto.

"One thing about business today," Mr. Tyler was saying, "they can't operate without insurance. When nobody downtown would listen, I figured that if I told Mid-City about the rotten cabs, they'd either get rid of Gold Star or make them clean up their act, as the young folks say."

"Only there was no Mid-City," Nancy said, beginning to understand.

"Right. But I thought it out. Expose Mid-City, and Gold Star would have to get another insurance company. To get one, they'd have to fix up their cabs. So that's the route I took."

"So you called me again telling me to talk to Mrs. Harvey," Ann said.

"Yes. I found out Brownley and Reston had paid Vera's bills themselves. If they did *that*, it meant they'd gone to Mid-City earlier to take care of the bills and found out it was phony then and there. But they've paid everybody's bills and have never said a word to anybody. They're as crooked as the Mid-City guys."

"So there *have* been other accidents?" Nancy asked to be certain.

"Minor ones, mainly with Crimson Oaks people. But Gold Star's got to be put out of business. And I'd like to be there when it happens. I'd give anything to know what they're doing in that basement."

Nancy frowned. "I thought you said it was empty."

"No, I said they closed it off," Mr. Tyler

corrected her. "Before I left shipments of sealed boxes started coming in. Brownley stashed them downstairs. And he signed for the delivery of a brand-new air compressor. The garage had needed one for months. But where'd it go? Down to the lower level, and that was the last I saw of it."

"Interesting," Nancy said.

"I just hope they don't discover that Jim Dayton is my grandson. They're crooks and they're hurting people, Ms. Granger. I was trying to stop them, that's all."

"I know you were," answered Ann, smiling at him. "And we're grateful for your help. May we call you again if we have any more questions?"

"Sure thing."

"He's a nice man," Ann said as they went back to the parking lot. "He had no idea what he was getting into."

Nancy wondered what she had gotten into and what was on the lower level of that garage that she'd have to investigate.

"Nancy Nickerson" made even more money her second night on the job because she turned in her cab at twelve. To her surprise, another man was sitting in for Brownley. "He had some business," the stranger told her.

Perfect, Nancy thought. She went back to her locker to get her other jacket before deciding what to do next. When she got there, she ran into Jim Dayton.

"Hi, remember me?" Nancy said.

"How could I forget?" he said, obviously happy to see her. "Just getting off?"

"Yes, how about you?"

"Yep. I worked late tonight, and boy, am I beat," he said. "Don't have to keep it up for much longer, though. Only two more weeks."

"Well, I hope you make it," Nancy said as she closed her locker door. And she meant it—in more ways than one. She wondered what would happen to him if the Gold Star management discovered that he was Tom Tyler's grandson.

"Good night now," she said.

"So long," he said.

Nancy returned to her car to wait until she was sure the cabs on the midnight shift had all left.

She sat in the car for forty-five minutes. Then, rather than walk all the way around the block to Gold Star, she cut through the dark alley separating it from the car wash.

Back on the street she saw that the rollup door was down. The office was empty, and the inside parking area appeared to be dimly lit. The midnight shift had hit the streets.

As Nancy sneaked into the building, she heard voices in the back of the parking area. Brownley's was one of them. The other brought goose pimples: Reston! She'd never forget his voice. Scurrying between two parked cabs, Nancy got as close to the two men as she could and peeked over the cars' hoods. She could also see someone hiding in the shadows.

It was Jim Dayton!

Reston was opening the rear door of a cab whose engine was running. "A beautiful sight, isn't it?" he said, pointing to something in the back. Nancy tried, but she couldn't see inside the cab.

Brownley grinned. "I'm just glad you didn't have any trouble. From here on, we're in clover. Which reminds me, Chicago's been holding a big shipment for us, waiting for us to clear up this mess. Okay if I tell them to send it?"

"Might as well. After Granger talks—and I promise, she will—our troubles will be over."

Nancy smiled grimly. If they thought Ann would tell who her source was, they were in for a surprise.

"We can get back on schedule," Reston was saying. "Open the door. The sooner I get downstairs, the better."

Brownley removed a ring of keys from his belt as Reston got back into the cab. "What about the Drew kid?" the dispatcher asked.

"What about her? We don't need to worry about her. She hasn't found out anything yet, and she never will. We're too smart for her."

Nancy wasn't sure whether to be relieved or insulted.

"Call me when you're ready to bring the cab

up again," Brownley said. "Oh, Mac may show up while you're down there, but he always comes the back way."

Nancy heard the jingle of keys, then watched as a section of the side wall at the rear slid open silently. A peculiar odor started wafting through the garage, but Nancy was too busy plotting her next step to identify it. There was a back way to the lower level! She had to find it!

She saw Jim slip outside, and as soon as the cab disappeared through the doorway, she made her move. Hurrying back outside and slipping around the side of the building, she cut through the alley again.

She patted the concrete wall as she moved toward the rear of the garage. The other door must be at the back. She took another step and walked smack into Jim Dayton.

"What are you doing here?" he whispered.

"I could ask you the same thing." Suddenly Nancy froze. There was someone directly behind her! Were they both going to be caught?

Chapter
Thirteen

S<small>HHH</small>! I<small>T</small>'<small>S JUST</small> me," came a whisper behind her. "Would you please tell me what you're doing groping around walls in the dark?"

Nancy spun around. "Ned! What are you doing here? What—what are you wearing?" The whole length of him was a soft white blur.

"A uniform. I've got a job at the car wash. This is my second night. I saw you last night when you took your cab through."

Nancy was so stunned that she spluttered. "Why didn't you say something?"

"I'm not supposed to chat with the customers. 'Get 'em in, get 'em out,' they told me. I knew you wouldn't be satisfied with a simple 'Good evening. Can I interest you in the hot wax?' So I ducked you."

"Okay. But why a job *there*, Ned?"

"Somebody's got to keep an eye on you. You keep sticking your head into nooses. I'm here to make sure no one slaps the horse out from under you."

"My hero," Nancy said and gave him a quick kiss.

"Hey, what's going on here?" Jim cut in.

"Oh, Jim, this is my boyfriend, Ned."

"Why are you investigating this place?" Jim asked, truly puzzled.

"It's a long story. All I can say now is that I've spoken to your grandfather."

"Did he send you out here to spy on me?" Jim asked. He was beginning to get angry.

"Not at all," Nancy said. "I'm looking out for something else. . . ."

But this was not the time for polite chatter.

"Look, this is getting more dangerous by the minute, so be careful," Nancy said. "Brownley and Reston have something going on in the basement."

"Hey, that's *my* line. I was going to tell you in the morning," Ned responded.

"Tell me what?"

"There's a lot of traffic in and out of there, especially after midnight. Guys driving in. And starting around one—it's almost that now—you can hear odd sounds from inside."

"What kind of odd sounds?" Nancy asked.

"Some kind of machine," Ned said. "It reminds me of a power mower, the same kind of buzz."

"It's probably the air compressor," Jim put in.

"Ann and I talked to Tom Tyler, Jim's grandfather, who used to be the mechanic here," Nancy said to Ned. "He told us about the lower level."

Ned nodded. "I should have remembered that myself. I used to park here when I was taking CPR at the Y. I could always find a spot on the lower level because most people went up instead of down."

"Mr. Tyler said Brownley and Reston closed it off and something fishy's been going on down there ever since," Nancy said.

"That's what I'm trying to figure out," Jim told them. "My grandfather just can't seem to forget all this. And I thought, while I'm working here, maybe I could put his suspicions to rest."

"Hey!" Ned grabbed Nancy's shoulders. "Before I forget, guess who uses the other half of the street level? Right next to Gold Star? Fleet's Courier Service. It's one of the businesses that uses white vans! And Gold Star's mechanic takes care of the cabs as well as the vans."

Nancy's mental wheels began to spin. "How very convenient," she said dryly.

"I think they have a basement level. If they do, it may be possible to get into Gold Star's basement through Fleet's," Jim suggested.

"I've thought about that, too. Want to take a look?" Nancy asked.

"I'd love to, but I have to get home—and right now," Jim said as he glanced at his watch. "Sorry, you guys. Look, maybe we'll get a chance to work together on this before I have to go back to school. Nice to meet you, Ned."

As soon as Jim left, Ned said, "Nancy, don't try it without me, understand? I leave at two, when the Gold Star guys take over. We can—"

"What do you mean, the Gold Star guys take over?"

"The dispatcher's worked out a deal with my boss. They close the wash to the public at two and run the cabs through."

"Every night?" Nancy asked, puzzled.

"I guess so."

Nancy leaned against the wall. "That's funny. Brownley told me that if the cab was dirty at the end of my shift, to run it through your place. If he tells all the drivers that, what's left to wash?"

"I don't know, but I've got to run. There goes a customer in the front. Promise me you won't do anything without me, okay?"

"I promise. The Mustang's parked in the public garage. Second level. I'll wait there for you."

"Deal." Ned bent down and kissed her. Then he sprinted into the gaudy glare of the car wash.

When he had disappeared inside, Nancy trotted around the block. There was no reason she couldn't just look inside Fleet's from the street. She wouldn't go inside, just look.

Fleet's rollup door was open halfway. Stooping to peer under it, Nancy saw a line of vans backed against the side walls. Some were larger than others, but they were all white and all had aerials for two-way radios. A glassed-in office, similar to the one next door at Gold Star, was tucked just inside the door.

Nancy scooted across to the other side and squinted at the door of the office. Above it was a sign: Fleet's Courier Service. P. Reston, Proprietor. This was getting better and better!

Nancy glanced at her watch, wondering if she should wake her father's secretary to ask if the firm used Fleet's. No, it was after one. It could wait. It was even more tempting to call Ann. The reporter kept weird hours, and she might still be up.

Dashing past Gold Star, Nancy darted into the alley. She'd get the Mustang and find a phone.

Then she heard a sound behind her. Someone else had walked into the alley.

Reston. Nancy stepped back, pressing against the side of the garage. Reston walked across the mouth of the alley to an old car parked alongside the car wash. He opened the trunk, took something out, and then headed back toward the entrance of Gold Star.

Hugging the shadows, Nancy slithered along the wall toward the car he'd just left. This was not the Buick he had driven the night before. In fact—

She tried the door on the driver's side. It was unlocked. Opening it just long enough for the ceiling light to come on, Nancy checked the interior. This was the car Reston had driven when he had kidnapped her!

Maybe I should check the trunk, she thought, removing the lock pick from her wallet. In less than fifteen seconds she had it open. Using her penlight was chancy but worth the risk if she found something important.

As it was, the contents were certainly interesting—several boxes of blank hack licenses, and the kind of dated stickers that were glued on the windshield of taxis after they had passed inspection.

Wedged in the corner was an unopened box marked Fragile. Nancy's curiosity got the best of her. She leaned in and played her penlight across the printing on its side: "Nature Under Glass. Fragile. This End Up." Nancy tried to pull it toward her. It was surprisingly heavy.

You're getting sidetracked, Drew, she told herself. Maybe it was a present for his wife or something. The important discoveries were the hack licenses and the inspection stickers.

Suddenly Nancy heard someone stepping from the sidewalk into the alley. She glanced up and realized with horror that it was Reston. Stooping quickly, she eased the trunk down, hoping she could duck-walk back into the shadows beside the building.

But at that moment a cab came around the corner and signaled for the turn into the car wash. Midway through that turn, its headlights would sweep over Reston's car. Even if Nancy were lucky enough for Reston to miss seeing her crouching by his trunk, there was no way the cabbie could miss her. She was trapped.

Chapter

Fourteen

THERE WAS ONLY one thing for Nancy to do. She hadn't closed the lid of Reston's trunk because he might have heard it. Easing it up again, she hooked one leg over and folded herself inside, lowering the lid again. A few seconds later she heard Reston climb into the driver's seat and start the car.

Nancy held the trunk open slightly so she could watch where Reston drove. He pulled out on McConnell, drove to the end of the block, and turned right. When he approached the next corner, he began to slow. There was a traffic signal at that intersection, and Nancy prayed it had caught him. Reston came to a complete stop —and Nancy didn't wait to guess why. She raised the lid of the trunk.

Down the street, a pair of headlights cut a

yellow path through the night as a car turned from McConnell and came toward them. The driver might be able to see her, but there was nothing she could do about it. Nancy scrambled out, keeping the trunk lid low, lowered it, and took off for the sidewalk. The light changed, and Reston disappeared around the corner. He hadn't spotted her!

Nancy stepped into the shadow of the awning of a shoe-repair shop. The car approaching the intersection slowed. Was it following her? Nancy tensed, then sighed with relief when she saw Ned in the driver's seat.

"Boy, am I glad to see you!" she said, hurrying around to the passenger side.

"Nancy Drew, have you flipped? What were you doing?"

"Looking to see what was in his trunk. Ned, that was Reston—the man who snatched me out of the Grand that day," she said, climbing in beside him.

"One ride with him wasn't enough?" Ned shook his head with exasperation. Then he reached over and pulled her close. "You drive me crazy sometimes. What did you find that was worth getting trapped for?"

"Cab inspection stickers, for one. That's how Gold Star's been able to keep such rattletraps on the road. They don't go through inspection at all."

"Which means someone in the Department of

Licenses and Inspections is being paid off. That's serious and worth going to a lot of trouble to hide."

"Uh-huh," Nancy said. "There were blank hack licenses in the trunk, too. Honest people have to fill out an application downtown, pay good money, and wait to get one. Brownley's passing out the things as if they're business cards. I know, I got one."

"Then we're talking about more than one person being on the receiving end of bribe money. When this gets out, it's going to rip the city apart!"

Nancy set her jaw. "That's just too bad. They're trying to rip my dad apart, aren't they?" Then Nancy's good humor returned. "Say, how'd you get away from the car wash so fast? And weren't you going to meet me at my car?"

"Nothing was happening, so I asked the boss if I could leave early. I was going to grab something to eat at the all-night deli before I met you to check out the courier service."

"Oh." Nancy winced. There was no way she could avoid telling him she had taken a short look without him. "I—I sort of strolled past it. Guess what? Reston runs Fleet's," she said as they drove toward the deli.

That bit of news was enough to make Ned forget she was supposed to have waited for him. "You're kidding!"

"And couriers swarm all over Judiciary Square

every day. There were two or three in and out of Ms. Hanson's office while I was looking for a bug. I don't know if any of them are from Fleet's, but of course I'll check it out."

A sudden thought skittered around in Nancy's mind, but it disappeared before she could capture it. She couldn't even imagine what had triggered it. At last she decided she'd better just relax and let the thought come back in its own time.

Ned stopped at the deli and bought sandwiches for Nancy and himself. They gobbled them down on their way back.

As they turned onto McConnell, Nancy groaned. "Will you look at that? I thought Fleet's was open around the clock! *Now* how can we check it out?"

Ned pulled up to the curb, and they climbed out, staying hidden behind the car so they could observe what was happening. Fleet's Courier Service was dark and locked tight as a drum. But Gold Star's garage appeared to be alive with activity. Nancy and Ned crept closer, using shadows for cover. Reston, Brownley, and a couple of drivers in white jackets with "Fleet's" stenciled on the backs were busily jockeying taxis around inside, as if making room for something.

"Well, now we know where the couriers are. Those cabs are new," Nancy whispered. "Maybe it's part of the shipment Brownley was talking about."

As they watched, a couple of cabs were driven next door to the car wash. As they drove through the bay doors, the lights went out. Anyone passing by would have thought the place was closed. "See?" Ned said.

"This is crazy," Nancy said. "Those cabs looked perfectly clean."

"Well, I warn you, this will go on for the next forty-five minutes. There's nothing more we can do tonight. We'll have to try tomorrow night, okay?"

Nancy hated to give up. She'd been primed to search for the route to the basement, but what Ned said made sense. They'd be risking discovery if they tried it with all those people around.

"Okay. Tomorrow night," she said. "I guess it's just as well." Suddenly she was very tired.

Ned drove her around to her car. They spent a leisurely few minutes saying good night, and then they each drove home.

Nancy went in the back door as usual, but didn't turn on the light in the kitchen. Her goal was bed, so she checked the lock, then walked straight through the darkened kitchen and up the stairs. That was why she didn't see her father's note on the refrigerator until the next morning.

It was the worst news she could have gotten. Carson Drew's pretrial hearing had been moved up. It was now scheduled for that very afternoon!

* * *

"Can they do that, Dad?" Nancy asked, horrified. She'd just come down for breakfast and read the note.

"I'm surprised that they moved it up," he admitted. "But it's not that unusual. I take it you haven't found anything to use to clear me?"

"We've found out a lot of things, and there aren't as many holes in the jigsaw puzzle as there were when we started." She told him about the discovery she had made the night before, thanks to the contents of Reston's trunk.

"But the most important piece is missing —how they framed you. I have an idea, but I need to get the proof."

Carson got up from the table. "All right. Keep at it, and please don't worry. Pretrial isn't the end of the world."

"Honest, Dad?" Nancy asked. She felt desolate at having let him down.

"Honest. Oh, by the way, I brought my associates up to date last night on what you're doing."

"You didn't tell them about my working at Gold Star, did you?"

"Yes. If they're going to defend me, they're entitled to know how the investigation is going. Will you be in court today?"

"Of course."

"Good." Her father managed a tight smile. "I can use the support. Courtroom C at two o'clock. And Leonard runs a tight court. He starts on time. I'm off. See you at two."

116

Nancy hurried up the stairs. She glanced through the notes she had made about the case and tossed them into a large tote bag. If she got lucky and found the answers she needed before two o'clock, she'd be prepared.

Suddenly the obvious answer to one of her problems hit her. "Of course! Mr. Tyler!" she said out loud.

She looked up his number and dialed it. "Mr. Tyler, this is Nancy Drew. I'm embarrassed that I didn't think to ask you this yesterday. Is there another way to get down to the lower level of the garage?"

"Hmmm. Besides the ramp they closed off?"

"Yes."

"Let me think." There was a long pause. Nancy had to force herself not to tell him to hurry. She closed her eyes and waited.

"Well, there may be. It's been a long time, so I'm not sure."

"Tell me anyway," Nancy said, prompting him.

"When the parking garage first opened, there were attendants who took your car and parked it for you. They used a conveyor elevator to get up and down to the different levels."

"A conveyor elevator?"

"It's like one long, moving ladder. All it would have is platforms big enough for your feet, and handholds. If you hop on it from one side, it would take you up—"

"And on the other side, you'd go down," Nancy interrupted excitedly. "But they don't use parking attendants anymore. Would the electricity still be on?"

"I doubt it. But if the conveyor's still there—if they didn't dismantle it, I mean—it would be stationary. You might be able to climb down it."

"It's worth a try," Nancy said. "Mr. Tyler, thank you so much."

She hung up immediately and called Ned. The line was busy, so she dialed Bess. "Oh, it's you," her friend said. She didn't sound very happy to hear from Nancy.

"Listen, Bess," Nancy said hurriedly. "They've moved my dad's pretrial hearing to today—"

"What?"

"Two o'clock this afternoon. Will you let Ann know and get her there on time? He's going to need a cheering section, and I know she'll want to be there."

"She's not at home," Bess said. "I figured you'd know where she was, since you two have gotten so tight."

"Huh?" Nancy said.

"Well, you obviously didn't want me along last night. I know she's bright and fun and all, but we've known each other—"

Fear pierced Nancy. "Bess, what do you mean I didn't want you along last night?"

"Well, what else could I think? Your message was as plain as day."

Nancy gritted her teeth. "What message, Bess?"

"You didn't leave a message for Ann last night?"

"What message, Bess?"

Sudden panic made her friend's voice squeaky. "Ann said you'd left a message at the *Morning Record* that you wanted her to wait for you in the newspaper parking lot at eleven last night. You wanted her to come alone, and you'd pick her up in your cab."

Nancy shivered, chilled to the bone. "They're on to me," she said. "They know I drive a cab. Somehow I blew my cover."

"Oh, no!" Bess said.

"That's not the worst. Reston was showing my dispatcher something in the back seat of a cab last night. And he said something about 'after Granger talks.' It must have been Ann in the cab!"

"Nancy, call the police!"

"I don't have any proof! I didn't actually see her. They aren't going to raid what they think is a reputable business on my say-so."

"What can we do?"

"Meet me at the parking garage, Bennett Street entrance, in half an hour. Reston drove the cab down to the basement. She may still be there."

"I'm on my way," Bess said and hung up.

Ned's line was still busy. Desperate, Nancy asked an operator to break in. "This is an emergency!" she cried.

The operator must have heard the panic in her voice, because she gave her no argument.

After an interminable wait, the operator came on again. "Sorry. There is no one on the line. It must be out of order. I'll report it."

It's off the hook, Nancy thought. Well, there was nothing she could do about it. It was time to go. With or without Ned, she would have to get into that basement in broad daylight.

Chapter

Fifteen

NANCY SPENT THE drive to the parking garage trying to figure out how she had slipped up. How could she have blown her cover? Bess was waiting at the Bennett Street entrance when she arrived, so Nancy decided to think about it later.

"Where's Ned?" Bess asked.

"I couldn't get him. I'm pretty sure his phone is off the hook. Hannah said she'd go and get him for me."

"Okay. What are we doing?"

"First we find a conveyor elevator."

"A what?"

Nancy explained as they trotted toward the enclosure that had served as the attendants' booth. It seemed logical that the conveyor would be somewhere near it.

"Here it is!" Nancy said.

It was behind the booth—no more than an air shaft with a structure inside that was precisely what Mr. Tyler had described. Nancy aimed her penlight into the space below. With luck, she'd be able to climb down. If her luck held, she'd wind up on Gold Star's side of the basement.

"Nancy, are you sure about this?" Bess asked. Her normally pink complexion was very pale.

"I'm sure. I've got to find Ann, as well as get proof that Brownley and Reston were behind the frame-up against my dad." Nancy pulled a long chain from under her sweater. Hanging from it was a whistle.

"What's that for?" Bess asked.

"Help, that's what. You stay here. If you hear this whistle before Ned gets here, scream your head off. Do whatever you have to to get help. If Ned gets here and you haven't heard me blow this, send him down."

Bess shook her head stubbornly. "I'm going with you. I'm scared, but I want to, so let's not waste time arguing about it."

Nancy hugged her. She knew it would be more sensible to leave Bess as a lookout, but she couldn't pass up the chance to have her along for moral support. "Thanks, Bess," she said. "Well, let's go."

It was a scary climb. The belt kept swaying, and after a certain point, Nancy felt as if she were climbing into a black hole, groping for the next place to put her feet. Above her, Bess peered nervously down into the darkness.

At the bottom, however, Nancy could see fairly well. On her right was a concrete block wall and a closed door. But on her left, light spilled over a row of boxes stacked six high.

Nancy helped Bess to the bottom and signaled for her to stand still.

Bess wrinkled her nose. "What's that smell?" she whispered.

It was the same smell Nancy had caught when Brownley had opened the door upstairs for Reston's cab. She was in Gold Star territory. And the smell was paint.

Nancy crossed to the door in the concrete wall and turned the knob. If it was a closet, they might have imprisoned Ann Granger in there.

But it was a workshop. Two-way radios and other mysterious electronic equipment filled shelves along the back wall. Several large tape decks and a pair of cassette players sat on a worktable. There were also electric drills and polishers.

In a bookcase just inside the door were hundreds of cassette tapes, neatly shelved and cataloged. A file cabinet was in a corner, and one drawer was hanging open.

Bess stuck her head in, and her eyes went round with wonder.

"This must be Fleet's side of the basement," Nancy whispered.

"Why would a courier service need tape-editing equipment? That's what that is." Bess pointed to a device on the table.

Nancy nodded toward the bookcase full of cassettes. "I wonder if any of those have my father's voice on them."

"Why don't I check this side of the basement?" Bess whispered. "You check the other side."

"Okay. It's a long shot, but my back's against the wall."

"Come get me if you need me." Bess crossed to the file cabinet and dug in.

Her nose twitching from the smell of paint, Nancy went back to the other side. A row of stacked boxes was the only thing preventing her from seeing what Gold Star had stored in there.

She pushed against one stack. It didn't move. Whatever was in the boxes was heavy. She might have to climb up to see over them.

Moving quietly, Nancy walked the length of the boxes and found a space perhaps a foot-and-a-half wide between the last stack and a round concrete column. She turned sideways and squeezed through the narrow space.

At first, everything looked perfectly normal. Shiny new cabs were parked along the opposite wall. A row of passenger cars was backed against the boxes. It was very quiet and still.

Then Nancy heard the big door being pulled

open upstairs. She was tempted to slip behind the boxes again, but there wasn't time.

She ducked, her heart pounding, as a car roared down from the street level. It pulled in from her right and stopped. Two car doors slammed.

Brownley said, "Beautiful! Beautiful, Mac! We'll keep this one out of sight down here until it's time to move it. No way am I putting any paint on this baby. Wish I could keep it myself. But next time, remember—no daytime deliveries."

Nancy lifted her head high enough to see. The dispatcher stood talking to a stranger and peeling bills off a wad of money in his hand.

"We'll change the numbers on the engine block tonight, switch plates, and send it on to Freddie day after tomorrow. Here's a thousand. You done good, Mac, boy."

So that's what this is about, Nancy mused. Stolen cars!

The man counted the bills and crammed them into his pocket. "Looks like you guys are behind schedule," he said.

"A little. But we'll be moving them in and out of here double-time until we're caught up. We've got the paint, but we may have to buy another compressor so we can paint two at a time."

"Good idea."

"Mac, can you come back tonight and help us take some of these through the car wash?"

"Sure. One-thirty, okay?"

"Fine. Run them through twice," Brownley said. "This new paint doesn't wash off as easily."

"If you say so. Let's get back to the money-making business. What kind of car do you want next?" the man asked.

"Come on back up to the office and I'll show you the list. Ever steal a Jaguar, Mac, boy?" With a hand on the stranger's shoulder, he led him toward the exit ramp.

Once they were out of sight, Nancy stood up. The latest arrival was a beautiful white Mercedes. She tiptoed over to get a closer look. The ignition wires were dangling beneath the dashboard. I was right, Nancy thought. It had been stolen.

She checked the other passenger cars. None had license plates. Seventeen of the twenty had loose ignition wires. Brownley had a steal-to-order business going here!

At the opposite end of the garage, a Dodge, its windows, grille, and bumpers covered with paper, glistened under a bright light. Nancy touched a fender. The paint was still wet. And there was Mr. Tyler's compressor. They used it to spray a stolen car Gold Star gold so it could be disguised until enough time had passed to sell it safely.

Nancy gazed at the row of cars now disguised as cabs. It was quite a collection—American cars, German, Japanese. The fourth from the end looked familiar. Nancy crossed to it, her heart tap-dancing in her chest. There was a slit in the back seat, and on the dashboard, a red, quarter-sized blob. Her nail polish. Ned's car!

From behind her, Nancy heard a muffled groan. Startled, she whirled around. The sound had come from a wire enclosure beside the compressor.

She hurried over to it. At first all she saw in it were car batteries, Gold Star roof lights, a trash barrel, and stacked cans of motor oil.

The sound came again, but louder. Something rolled into view, and Nancy gasped. Ann Granger lay on her back, bound hand and foot, tape across her mouth. She stared at Nancy, her eyes unfocused.

"Shhh!" Nancy said. Ann blinked groggily.

The door of the enclosure was secured with a hefty padlock. Nancy took out her set of picks and went to work on it. She knew it wouldn't be easy. Time stretched. Nancy was in agony, working as fast as she could.

Just as the hasp pulled free with a click, Ann made an urgent sound deep in her throat. Too late Nancy realized that the click had not come from the lock, but from behind her. She turned around and found herself facing the business end of a silver-plated automatic pistol.

Chapter

Sixteen

"THAT OUGHT TO hold you." Brownley tightened the last knot around Nancy's ankles, after tying her hands behind her back.

Reston, lips stretched in a slash of a smile, squatted beside her, the gun to her temple. With the other hand, he snatched the tape from Ann's mouth. "So you finally woke up, Granger. Good. Let's not waste each other's time. Who's the snitch in our organization?"

"I don't know," Ann said, speaking with difficulty.

Suddenly Nancy noticed Jim Dayton lurking in the shadows. He was holding a baseball bat. She felt a small twinge of hope that they just might get out of there alive.

Meanwhile, Reston was not sympathetic. "Either you give me the name, Ms. Granger, or our young friend here joins the angels."

"Honestly, I don't know who it is," Ann said. "Whoever it was just left messages for me. Please, I don't feel well."

"The stuff we gave you will do that," Reston said. He jabbed her in the side. "Come on, Miss Investigative Reporter, talk—or you'll feel a lot worse. Who's the snitch?"

"She doesn't know," Nancy said, wondering if Bess was safe. "If she did, would she have fallen for that trick of yours to meet you at the Grand Cinema? Stop poking her! She hasn't been out of the hospital that long, remember?"

"Hey, Reston, she don't look so good." Brownley peered down into Ann's face. "You sure that stuff you used to put her out was all right?"

"What difference does it make?" Reston turned the gun on Nancy again. "*You* tell me who it is, then," he said and raised his arm, as if to hit her.

Ann squirmed to sit upright. "Please, don't hurt her!"

Unfortunately, Jim picked that moment to charge forward. He went to slam Reston with the bat, but Brownley was quick to intercept. He spun Jim around and punched him so hard that he knocked him out.

"I see you ladies have engaged some help," Reston said and nodded a thanks to Brownley.

Nancy peered at Jim lying on the floor, and her heart sank. She recovered quickly and said, "Don't waste your breath, Ann." Nancy looked Reston in the eye. "He's going to kill us, whether he gets the name or not. He has to. We know too much."

"You also talk too much," Reston growled.

"It must be a very successful business," Nancy went on, "considering the trouble you've gone to to protect it. How much have you been pulling in?"

"No harm in my telling you. You won't be passing it along. About a million a year."

"Pretty good," Nancy said. "Certainly enough to spread some around to people who can help keep you in operation. How many people are on your payroll?"

Reston shrugged. "Ten. They're cheap, all things considered. A hack inspector here, a police records clerk there. They don't ask for much. But they're a big help."

"And the judge? He was about to blow it for you, wasn't he?"

"Yes, which was unfortunate. It was very handy having someone who could tip us off about search warrants, or secret indictments that would put certain friends behind bars. No matter. We're grooming someone to take his place. Now—" He placed the gun against her temple.

"One last thing," Nancy said, her mouth dry.

She had to play for time. "What were you holding over the judge's head?"

Reston grinned. "Gambling debts. For every tip he gave us, we knocked ten thousand off his bill."

"How much was framing my father worth?"

"Fifty thousand. And it worked. Your daddy's going to jail, little girl."

"Sooner or later, you will, too—for first-degree murder."

"What's she talking about?" Brownley stared at Reston. "You killed Renk? You said it wasn't you! You said somebody had done us a favor!"

"So I lied. After little Ms. Drew got away from me, I went to relieve Casper out near the judge's place. And who shows up? Ms. Drew again."

"You didn't tell me about that!" Brownley said, eyeing his partner as if he were seeing him for the first time.

"I don't report to you. I could hear Renk beginning to cave in loud and clear. He had to go. What do you care?"

"If he doesn't care," Nancy said, "he should. You made him an accessory to murder."

"Wait a minute! I didn't know anything about it!" Brownley's ruddy complexion had turned ashen.

"Maybe not. But you will know about ours," Nancy pointed out. "If he kills us, you might as well have pulled the trigger. He tried to kill us once before."

"No, I didn't, girlie. If you mean that car bomb, that was a mistake. The bozo I hired did it all wrong. Why would I kill her when I needed information from her."

Brownley backed out of the wire enclosure. "I don't want anything to do with murder, Reston. You kill them and you're on your own."

For the first time, Nancy saw uncertainty in Reston's icy gray eyes. "Maybe you're right." He backed out of the cage and slammed the door. "You come up with me. We'll talk."

Brownley looked worried as he secured the padlock.

As soon as they were out of sight, Nancy began looking around for a means of escape.

"I'm so sorry, Nancy," Ann said. "They fooled me. I thought it was you driving that cab. I opened the door to get in, felt a stinging in my arm—and that's all I remember."

"Forget it. My dad's hearing is this afternoon. If we don't get out of here, we'll probably wind up in the nearest river and my dad'll wind up in jail." She peered out of the enclosure. "And it doesn't look like Jim will be able to help us."

Scooting over to the wall, Nancy leaned her back against it and pushed herself to a standing position. She then reached into the trash barrel for one of the oil cans and tilted it toward her wrists. There wasn't much left in it, but what little there was oozed over her hands, coating them with the thick fluid.

It took draining the dregs from two more cans before her wrists were slippery enough for her to work the cord off. She then untied her feet and freed Ann.

But their problems were far from over. The enclosure was locked, and Nancy had no idea what happened to the pick she had been using when she was caught.

"Pssst!"

Nancy's head snapped up. Bess, on all fours, scuttled over to the wire cage. Her eyes were twice their usual size. She looked heavier than usual, too.

"Nancy! Ann! You're okay!" She looked at the lock with alarm.

"My pick set may be out there on the floor somewhere," Nancy said. "See if you can find it."

Bess pawed through the trash outside the door. "Here it is. Now what?"

"The weave of the wire is too small for me to get my hands through," Nancy said. "You'll have to get it open for us."

"Me?" Bess swallowed and squared her shoulders. "Okay. Tell me what to do."

Nancy prompted her, forcing patience and encouragement into her tone. It seemed to take forever, but after a struggle, the lock clicked open and the door came ajar.

"Quick! This way," Nancy said and started for the row of boxes.

"Uh, I think I'm going to need help." Ann's voice was weak. Her legs seemed to be even weaker. "It's that stuff they gave me."

Nancy and Bess looked at each other in dismay, then moved back to her side. Awkwardly, they maneuvered her between the cars and pushed and shoved her through the space at the end of the boxes.

At the bottom of the conveyor, Bess shook her head. "No way she can make it up this thing, Nancy. You go on. I'll stay with her."

Ann shook her head. "No! Leave me. You've got what you need to help Carson. Get out of here. Go to him."

Nancy would have loved to do just that, but she felt responsible for her two friends and Jim. It was certain that if they didn't get away, Reston would be glad to shoot them.

She looked at the door to the courier service. "Let me check and see if we can slip out from Fleet's side. If we can make it to the street level, we can hide in one of the vans until the coast is clear."

"No." Bess's voice was firm. "I'll do that. You go on. Here." She yanked the tail of her blouse from her jeans and pulled a bulky envelope from under it.

"I thought you looked awfully lumpy," Nancy said. "What is it?"

"Cassettes of your dad's and the judge's

134

voices. The dummies had everything marked plain as day."

Nancy shook her head in amazement. "Bess, you've been super. I'll get help for you all as soon as I can."

"Wait," Bess said. "I've got something else for you. It—" She stopped. "What was that?"

The conveyor swayed and began to quiver. Someone was coming down!

Nancy thought fast. Maybe it was Ned—but she couldn't count on that.

"Come on!" she whispered. She grabbed Ann's right arm, Bess took the left, and they crossed to the door of Fleet's. Nancy yanked it open—and ran smack into Brownley.

Chapter

Seventeen

"GET IN HERE!" Brownley hissed and yanked them into the electronics workshop. He eased the door closed quickly, then cracked it just enough to see who was climbing down the conveyor.

While he was occupied, Bess snatched the envelope of evidence from Nancy's hand and crammed it back under her blouse. By the time Brownley said, "Mac's come back. Wonder why," the envelope was safely out of sight.

He closed the door and turned to face them. His skin was flushed, his eyes wide and staring. "Thought you were home free, didn't you? Well, you aren't!"

"You aren't, either, are you?" Nancy moved from beside Ann and walked slowly around the workshop. "What were you doing in here? Trying to remove incriminating evidence connecting you with the judge?"

Papers were strewn all over the floor. File drawers hung open. Tapes had been pulled from the shelves and lay at all angles. Bess would have been too smart to leave such a mess.

But the batch of papers Brownley was clutching really gave him away. Like a child caught with his hand in the cookie jar, he dropped them. "Shut up! You don't know what you're talking about," he growled.

"I think she does," Bess said, picking up Nancy's lead. "What she said over there sank in. They can get you for the judge's murder, and there's nothing you can do about it. Who's going to believe you didn't know Reston killed him?"

"But I didn't know!"

"Then why were you going to cut and run?" Ann asked. She was looking a little better.

Brownley ground his teeth. "I'm not going to jail for something I didn't do. Grand theft auto, that's one thing. I deal in stolen cars. I'm good at it. But I'm no killer, and I'm not taking the rap for Reston. I'm clearing out of here."

"What about us?" Nancy asked. "If you leave us here, that's four more murders they can get you for. Help us get out of here, and—"

"And what?" The door flew open—and Reston stepped in. "Mac told me you left as soon as I turned my back. Where'd *you* come from?" he asked, noticing Bess. Then he turned to his partner, his eyes like steel. "You were going to run out on me, weren't you, Brownley?"

Nancy snorted. The dispatcher was a possible ally, and against Reston they'd need all the help they could get. "He's not smart enough to run out on you," she said.

Brownley eyed her sharply. "I caught them trying to escape."

"Why make matters worse than they already are?" Nancy asked Brownley. "My boyfriend was hiding when you caught us the first time. He got us out of that cage and went up the conveyor to get the police. They're probably swarming all over the place by now."

Reston gave his nasty grin again. "Good try, little girl. But it won't work." He snatched the door open and shoved her back to the Gold Star side. Someone had moved one stack of boxes. Reston stepped through, then waited, gun drawn, for the rest of them to join him.

"Sit!" he ordered. "Until I decide what to do with you."

They sat down gingerly on the hard concrete, their backs against the unpainted cars. As Reston kept the gun trained on them, they waited. And waited. They were in a war of nerves.

Nancy knew they had to get away! Where was Ned? Suppose he hadn't been home after all!

After a half an hour Reston began to crack. He

started to pace and mutter. Another fifteen minutes, and his left eye began to twitch.

Finally he said, "I'm getting out of here. If there *are* police upstairs, which I doubt, you three will make fine hostages. The first sign of trouble," he snarled, wagging the gun toward Nancy, "and you get it first."

Nancy got up slowly, stiff from sitting so long. Then, from the corner of her eye, Nancy saw someone scurry between two cars. She almost fainted with relief. It was Ned! He was working his way toward them.

Reston beckoned to Nancy. "You. Come here. We're going upstairs. You'll be my shield."

"What about me?" Brownley asked.

"Take whichever one you want. Keep the other one between us."

As she edged toward Reston, Nancy saw Ned move closer. She hoped he'd stop there. Any closer, and he'd be exposed.

Then Ann caught Nancy's attention. The reporter's eyes were almost closed. She looked pale, but surprisingly, she winked at Nancy. She had seen Ned, too! Her eyes darted toward Bess, back to Nancy, then back to Bess again.

Nancy looked at Bess with a quick sidewise glance and became very still. Bess's lips were puckered. She puffed out her cheeks—once, then twice—and patted her chest.

The whistle! She was reminding Nancy of the whistle!

Nancy gave her a tight nod. Tensed for action, she waited.

Suddenly Ann moaned and began to crumple to the floor. Reston turned toward her.

Nancy moved in a blur of activity. Grabbing the chain around her neck, she yanked the whistle from under her sweater, put it in her mouth, and blew for all she was worth.

Reston whirled around. Nancy was balanced on one foot, ready for him. The other foot shot upward, the toe of her shoe slamming into the man's hand.

The gun arched toward the ceiling. As Reston grabbed his wrist in agony, Nancy's foot was in action again. This time she caught the point of his chin. His head snapped back, and he hit the floor as if he'd been struck by lightning.

Brownley had hesitated for a fraction of a second too long. He darted toward the door, but Ned tackled him. The impact slammed the dispatcher against the grille of one of the cabs. He was knocked cold.

"It worked!" Ned hugged Bess, then Nancy, before he bent to help Ann from the floor.

"Ned," the reporter said, "I have never been so glad to see anyone in my life. Nancy, you were terrific!"

"If it hadn't been for Bess," Nancy said, "I'd probably still be standing there like an idiot."

Ned took her hand. "I'm so sorry about that stupid phone! Hannah drove all the way over to tell me where you'd be. I got here as soon as I could."

"You were just in time," Nancy said, grabbing him in a bear hug. "And speaking of time, we've got to go!"

They all looked at Jim, who had only moaned when Nancy's whistle had sounded.

"Maybe he should stay here with me. George's car is right outside the entrance to Fleet's," Ned said. "You take it. I'll put these two in that cage and call the police."

Ann, leaning weakly against a Cadillac, managed a smile. "I'll stay, too. The way my legs are shaking, I'd just slow you down."

"Come on, let's go," Bess said, tugging the envelope from her blouse again.

Nancy started toward the door. "By the way, Ned, I've got a surprise for you."

"What?"

She turned and pointed. "There's your car."

He looked at it and made a strangled sound. "It's gold! Somebody's painted my baby gold! Why?"

"It's a long story," Ann said with a genuine smile. "Scram, Nancy. I'll tell him."

Nancy threw him a kiss and grabbed Bess. "Let's go." They sprinted through the opening in the stack of boxes. "Might as well cut through Fleet's," Nancy said. "I've seen enough Gold Star cabs today."

They had just skirted the worktable when

suddenly Nancy skidded to a stop and spun around.

"What? What?" Bess said.

"Something I just saw." Backtracking, Nancy went to the file cabinet. On the floor beside it was a box labeled "Nature Under Glass. Fragile." Sitting on top of it was a plastic bowl. Nancy picked it up and peered at its contents, her mouth falling open in astonishment.

"Ladybugs!" Bess exclaimed.

Nancy reached in and removed a few. "They aren't real. See what's in the box, will you?"

While her friend pried open the flaps, Nancy examined the ladybugs more closely. They were tiny, soft-plastic replicas with hollow undersides.

"There are paperweights in here," Bess said. Nestled in the box in protective cushioning were heavy glass domes, each with a different kind of flower embedded in it.

Nancy turned slowly and stared at the big drill on the worktable. "Drew, you are slipping," she murmured. "Bess, can you carry a couple of the paperweights?"

"Sure. Why? Nancy, it's after two!"

"I just found the bug I was looking for." She slipped the ladybugs in her pocket and picked up the drill. "Let's go."

"Well, since we're grabbing stuff," Bess said. She crossed behind the worktable and picked up the papers Brownley had dropped. "These must be valuable, or he wouldn't have pulled them out of the file."

"Good idea," Nancy agreed as they ran out. "The more proof we have, the better. It's a cinch Reston and Brownley will deny everything."

"Oh! I started to tell you before." Bess rooted in her pocket as they ran past startled couriers on the street level. "I don't know if it worked, but I slipped one of their minirecorders in my pocket. They had a lot of them."

She pulled it out as Nancy unlocked George's car. "It's still running!" she whooped, climbing in. "I've got everything they said on tape!"

"You're kidding!" Nancy started the engine and tore away from the curb. "Everything?"

"I was *behind* the boxes when they were talking about the judge," Bess said, buckling her seat belt. "But these little things have good mikes in them."

"In other words, we bugged *them!*" Nancy said, taking a corner on two wheels. "Oh, Bess, you're wonderful! Now if we can only get to court before Judge Leonard winds things—"

"Leonard?" Bess twisted in her seat. "The judge for your father's pretrial is Leonard?"

"That's right. Stanford Leonard, I think."

"Oh, no! Oh, Nancy! One of the cassettes was marked S. Leonard! The judge may be on Reston's payroll!"

Chapter

Eighteen

NANCY'S STOMACH DROPPED. "Reston said he had been grooming another judge to take my uncle's place."

"Then Leonard must be the one," Bess said.

"But Judge Leonard is one of the finest men on the bench! My dad said he wouldn't be surprised if Leonard ended up on the Supreme Court!"

"If the wrong thing's on that tape back there, he'll wind up in jail."

Nancy ran a yellow light and sped toward Judiciary Square. "Well, if he's in the enemy camp, there's one more stop I'd better make."

"Where?"

"My dad's office."

Poor Ms. Hanson almost jumped out of her skin when Nancy burst through the door. She had an envelope of money in her hand, and the coins went flying.

"Is it over?" the secretary cried. "Has Mr. Drew been bound over for trial?"

"I don't know," Nancy said and dashed into her father's office.

The object of her detour sat on her father's desk, twinkling in the sunlight. She picked it up to double check her theory. The ladybug was positioned directly under one of the tapered holes for pencils. It was the perfect place for a hidden mike. A bug in a bug!

On her way out, her eyes raked the secretary's desk. No paperweight.

"Oh, are you taking that home?" Ms. Hanson asked bewilderedly. "That's what I did with mine."

Quickly Nancy put a finger to her lips. She went back into her father's office, turned on his radio, and placed the paperweight in front of the speaker.

Ms. Hanson watched from the doorway, clearly confused. Nancy pulled her out and closed the door.

"How did you and my dad get those paperweights?" she asked softly.

"One of the messenger services passed them out when they first started business—a nice public-relations gesture. Mine had a pansy, my favorite, so I—"

"Passed them out?" Nancy interrupted. "To whom?"

"Everybody. They're all over the building. All over the square, for that matter."

Nancy gasped. "The whole of Judiciary Square?"

"Here and in the professional building—and that highrise full of attorneys a couple of blocks over. What's the matter?"

Nancy shook her head. "I don't have time to explain. Thanks, Ms. Hanson."

Something glinted in the thick brown carpet. Nancy bent down, picked up a dime, and dropped it into the secretary's hand as she started for her father's office again.

Suddenly she stopped short. Ms. Hanson was gathering the other change on her desk.

"Is that money for buying coffee supplies?" Nancy asked.

"Yes. Oh, will you do me a favor?" She opened the envelope and removed two twenty-dollar bills. "Keep that for your father. He put a fifty in because he didn't have anything smaller. That's his change."

Nancy felt as if the sun had just come out after a long, cold night. She checked the envelope. It was office stationery, with no writing on it. "How often does he contribute to the coffee fund?"

"Oh, every couple of weeks."

"And he just puts it in an envelope and leaves it for you?"

Ms. Hanson eyed her worriedly. "That's right. Do you feel all right, Nancy?"

Nancy leaned over and kissed her. "I feel fine, Ms. Hanson. For the first time in days, I feel *terrific!*"

She ran back into her father's office, grabbed the paperweight, and left.

Nancy had picked up Bess, and the two girls pelted through the halls of the courthouse as if they were trying for gold medals. People turned and stared, and a security guard shouted, "Hey!" and began to run after them.

"What took you so long?" Bess panted. "And what were you doing in that parking lot across the street from your dad's office? I could see you from here."

"Later," Nancy said as they burst through the doors of Courtroom C. Judge Leonard, stern and unsmiling, lifted his gavel and pounded on his desk. "Bailiff, remove these—"

Carson had stood at the disruption, his face appearing ten years older than when Nancy had last seen him. One look at her—and the broad smile on her face—and the years began to drop away. He knew she had done it.

"Stanford," he said, then corrected himself. "Sorry. Your Honor, this is my daughter, Nancy. And her friend Bess Marvin."

"Oh. Very well. Take seats, young ladies. I regret that you've arrived at this particular point in the proceedings. I am ready to make a judgment."

"Your Honor, please," Nancy said, moving down to the table at which her father and his associates sat. "I have a few items I'd like to offer into evidence, if that's the way to say it."

Judge Leonard frowned. "This is highly irregular. Mr. Drew, was this your idea?"

Nancy's father stood up. "You may or may not know, Your Honor, that my daughter is a detective."

The judge's brows flipped toward his hairline. "A detective?"

"She's been investigating the charges against me, and from the way she made her entrance, I assume she's met with some measure of success."

"I have—" Nancy looked back at Bess. "*We* have, Your Honor." Bess turned peach and grinned.

"I agree that this is highly irregular," Carson continued. "But if she's given a chance to present her evidence, we may save all of us a great deal of time and trouble."

Nancy watched the judge closely. His reaction at that point would determine how she began —whether she should consider him one of the rat pack or one of its victims.

"Very well," he said. "Present your evidence."

Nancy removed the paperweight from her pocket and held it up. "Defense exhibit A. I just removed this from my father's office. This is one of the foundations of the conspiracy against my father."

"A paperweight?" Judge Leonard said, with barely hidden impatience. "What bearing could it have? I have one like it. So has my secretary."

"Do they all have ladybugs on the flowers?"

"Yes, I believe they do."

Nancy beckoned to Bess, who knew exactly what to do. She took out the paperweights she had removed from the box and put them on the table. Nancy scooped up the ladybugs and spread them out. "Defense exhibit B," she said solemnly.

Then she took the heavy drill and, raising it above her head, smashed her father's paperweight.

Carson Drew leaned over. "Nancy, what are you doing?"

Without answering, Nancy brushed aside the chunks of glass and carefully removed the ladybug. Turning it over, she showed it to the judge.

His eyes went round, his mouth opening in dawning horror. "Let me see that," he said, and came down off the bench to stand beside her.

"There are microphones in all of the ladybugs," Nancy said. "Fleet's Courier Service drilled holes for pencil points into the tops of the paperweights and maneuvered the ladybugs down through one of the holes. Then they gave them away to judges, lawyers—"

"District attorneys," the district attorney added tightly.

"Across the street in the parking lot, you'll find a white Fleet's van with two flat tires," Nancy said. "I slashed them a few minutes ago. The van's full of electronic listening equipment and recording devices, and it's been picking up conversations all over Judiciary Square."

"Bailiff," Judge Leonard snapped, "get some officers and locate that van immediately! Is there anyone in it, Ms. Drew?"

"Yes, sir. After I punctured the tires, I jammed all the locks. He's stuck, just waiting to be picked up."

The bailiff ran up the aisle and out the door.

"They used the paperweight to tape my dad's voice," Nancy said, continuing.

Bess, the ever-ready assistant, slid the tapes out of the envelope and said, "Defense exhibit C." Then she darted back to her seat.

"We found these in the basement of Fleet's. You can see they're clearly marked—one with my father's name, one with Judge Jonathan Renk's, and one with both. They're building a library down there."

"And I imagine my name is on one of those volumes," the judge said, his face red with anger. "Get somebody to send the police to this place," he barked at the district attorney.

"They're probably already there, to pick up the men who're behind this. The owners of the Gold Star Cab Company."

"What's a cab company got to do with this?" the judge asked.

"Uh, if you don't mind, Your Honor, if I don't get exhibit—what is it? D?—on the table at this point, I'll lose my train of thought."

He smiled. "Then by all means go on."

Nancy handed her father the two twenty-dollar bills. "Ms. Hanson—that's my father's secretary —sent this. It's your change from the coffee money envelope, Dad."

He took it. "This could have waited, honey."

"I don't think so," Nancy said, holding up the envelope. "I'm told you make your contribution every couple of weeks."

Carson Drew nodded. "That's right. We all do. We—" He stopped, staring, then groaned. "The blank envelope. The *coffee* envelope. Is my face red!"

"One of Fleet's couriers simply removed a blank envelope from the stationery rack behind Ms. Hanson's desk," Nancy explained, "slipped the coffee money into it, and kept the one you'd handled."

"So simple. It was brilliant," Carson exclaimed.

"The couriers are in and out around the clock. I'm guessing one got into your office at night while the cleaning crew was there and typed Unc—I mean, Judge Renk's name on it."

"And Fleet's supplied the ten thousand dollars with which to implicate your father?" Judge Leonard said. "They could afford that?"

Nancy grinned. "That and more. Judge Leonard, do I have a story for you!"

Chapter

Nineteen

INCREDIBLE, ABSOLUTELY INCREDIBLE," Carson Drew said.

Everyone, Mr. Tyler and Jim Dayton included, was positioned in various stages of collapse in the Drew living room, stuffed to the gills. Hannah had fed them as if it were their last meal.

"All this was to hide a stolen car operation?" Carson asked.

"A million-dollar-a-year stolen car operation," Nancy emphasized. "They've been setting it up for years, bribing anyone who could keep the cab company front going—hack inspectors, licensing officers, police department record clerks."

"Some city officials are going to be very embarrassed," Ann said.

"It was a smooth operation," Ned said. "They'd bring in a stolen car and paint it gold."

He shuddered. "Then they'd slap a magnetic roof light on it, stencil Gold Star on its side, and leave it parked in the garage for a while."

"Then they'd take it through the car wash to get the water-based paint off and send it on its way—to a used-car lot." Nancy smiled. "And Ann's story threatened to expose it all."

"They needed an insurance company for Gold Star, so they set up the Mid-City cover," Ann said. "The only businesses Mid-City covered —on paper, that is—was Gold Star, Fleet's, and Freddie's Used Cars."

"But how'd they pull in Jonathan?" Carson asked.

Ned rolled over. He was lying on the floor. "Brownley told us after Nancy and Bess left. He and Reston met the judge at Pinebrook when they went to visit Mrs. Harvey. They had to stay on her good side."

"They saw how much he enjoyed playing cards and introduced him to some of their buddies," Ann supplied. "They let him win at first, and that's all it took. He began to lose. Soon he owed them a fortune."

"He tried the usual way out first," Ned said. "He borrowed it from the bank to pay them. But he kept losing—and wound up owing the banks and them, too."

"They finally reeled him in by advancing him the money to pay off all the loans," Nancy said sadly. "Then they let him work off the debt by passing along confidential information any time one of their people was about to get dropped on."

"Who thought up the paperweight bugs?" Mr. Tyler asked.

"Reston," Nancy answered. "Once they realized how valuable someone like the judge could be to the organization, they dreamed up the paperweights. Not only could they listen in and pick up information, they could use some things they heard for blackmail. Judge Leonard was on their list."

"For what?" Hannah asked.

"He checked himself into a mental hospital a few years back," Carson explained. "He'd just lost his wife and son in a car accident. He was suffering bouts of depression."

Ann sat up. "That was no secret! It's even in our files at the *Morning Record,* but Brownley and Reston didn't know it was common knowledge."

"They'd had such an easy time with Jonathan," Carson said with a sigh, "that they figured anyone they leaned on would fall into line."

"And once they thought someone they were paying was endangering their stolen car business by talking to Ann," Bess said, "they really put the pressure on—everyone."

"Only they didn't bargain on this little lady." Mr. Tyler patted Nancy's arm.

"And I thought I'd let you help *me* when I met

you in the alley that night," Jim put in. "Look who ended up helping whom. My head still hurts!"

Ned put his arm around Nancy. "It doesn't pay to underestimate Nancy Drew, private detective."

Nancy smiled, gazing from Ned to her father affectionately. She felt terrific. She had Ned at her side. She had two new friends—Ann and Jim—the gratitude of Jim's grandfather, Mr. Tyler, and she had just helped put the murderer of an old friend behind bars.

But the topper, the most important thing of all, was that she had cleared her father. She had just closed the most important case of her life!

Nancy's next case:

George Fayne has really been pushing herself, getting ready for a major international bicycle race. But as Nancy finds, her friend may have pushed herself into deadly danger!

Someone is threatening George's life. And Nancy finds too many people who want George out of the way. There's a racing rival who doesn't mind cheating, some KGB watchdogs of a Russian racer, and a girl who used to go out with George's boyfriend, Jon—and who'll stop at nothing to win him back.

Nancy finds herself in a desperate struggle to protect her friend—without even knowing where the danger is coming from! Can she save George? Find out in *NEVER SAY DIE,* Case #16 in The Nancy Drew Files℠.